One Fine Day

BY

ANNA SABLE

AuthorHouse™ UK
1663 Liberty Drive
Bloomington, IN 47403 USA
www.authorhouse.co.uk
Phone: 0800.197.4150

Published by AuthorHouse 01/19/2015

ISBN: 978-1-4969-9822-4 (sc)
ISBN: 978-1-4969-9821-7 (hc)
ISBN: 978-1-4969-9823-1 (e)

Cover photograph: Paulina Anna D'Offizi, Rome, 1936.

This book is printed on acid-free paper.

Un bel di vedremo

Madama Butterfly: Giacomo Puccini

"A wonderful fact to reflect upon, that every human creature is constituted to be that profound secret and mystery to every other."

Charles Dickens: *A Tale of Two Cities*

A Tale of Two Cities by Charles Dickens was the one of my mother's two favourite books. It is a tale of revolution, of relationships, of principles and of disappointments, of change of heart, for the better or for the worse. It tells of human actions and how they often belie human ideas or ideals, and how in the end actions will always speak louder than words, even in the beginning, some would say. That actions speak louder than words was moreover an article of faith for her.

It was a book after my mother's own heart, and it would, in time, reflect upon her own experience more than her first meeting with its pages had intimated to her.

The edition I now hold in my hands, and from which I quote, re-reading, as it were, with her eyes, is one I gave to her in 1961, on her birthday. On the title page, in my handwriting, in black ink, (the fountain pen I think was from her) I read: *To dear Mummy With all my love.*

HER STORY
1

I promised my mother that one day, in the unforeseeable future, as 'one day' represents, I would tell *her* tale.

I promised easily, full of anticipation and excitement at the prospects of the task. She had told me many tales from her life, which had been one full of adventure, giving her a wide experience of the world. There was much she refrained from telling me, a ten-year-old child, and which I believe she expected me to discover for myself in that envisaged time to come when she no longer lived.

She considered me her scribe, for whom she had made sacrifices in order that I be endowed with that gift of all gifts, a 'good education', and to whom the writing down, documenting and eternalizing of her existence would present no problem. From head, to hand, to paper, from thought to the written word in one fell swoop.

This unshaken, and unshakeable, belief in my educated capacities was, I realize it now, her true gift to me. Even though she pronounced her wish for immortality-in-words as an obligation she was laying on me for all the sacrifices she had made on my behalf, it never, strangely enough in the light, or perhaps I should say 'shadow', of other burdens of gratitude, felt that way. So that unwavering, predetermined belief, and my own promise to her that her tale would be told, have kept me mindful of the worthiness of writing.

In secret, she followed my literary efforts for several years – they were secret almost to my self, but carefully archived as the products of early youth often are. They were not locked away, our living arrangements made no room for a chest-of-drawers, with or without hidden compartments. And anyway, it was my mother who carried the keys to everything with a lock, and who needed to protect her tokens of an affluent past from prying eyes and thieving hands.

What I did have was a Victorian writing desk in mahogany, the key lost long ago. It was called a "desk", though it was more a box, reinforced with bronze corners and hinges. Inside you could keep writing paper and written papers. When opened, its sloping surface inlaid with moss-green leather was at just the right angle for writing. There was a curved hollow at the top for pens and a square hole for the silver-topped ink-pot of thick glass. It was made for travelling, in the days when travel and writing were indispensable to each other, and was an accoutrement of a certain class so that they could write where ever they might find themselves and keep their writings safe from the curiosity of strangers and familiars until ready to be despatched.

For the miniature desk was from that time of letter-writing and of diaries, a diary being one long letter to oneself or to the imagined world-at-large. It was also a place for keeping secrets, as its synonym *secretaire* suggests. I did not keep a diary but my first efforts at what is called creative writing were letters to someone I called Elizabeth.

The desk came into my eager hands because of my mother's unflagging desire to bring her gentlewoman's past into our drab present.

In the short interval of peaceful co-existence with our close-by outside world, when Anna's dream of a place of our own had finally materialized, and we had moved to London, no longer to wander the fair English countryside, she had quickly got acquainted with the neighbours. In this part of London the neighbours were very close, literally, stuck together, the houses built together in rows, and rows, and a bombed site intervening here and there provided a welcome gap of light and space to breathe. The old lady on the ground floor flat in the house next door, had taken a liking to me, and my mother feeling sorry for this lonely little lady, would send me in with chicken broth and other delicacies for the frail and aged.

It was always dark in there, and the gas-fire always hissed. The mantelpiece was crammed with old sepia-tinted photographs, the kind printed out on hardboard and decorated with the name and address of the photographer rather than that of the photographed. Which of them were of her was impossible to say. But there were no recent ones of anybody. So when she died it took a while to trace anyone who could take responsibility for her burial and the disposition of her worldly goods. The furniture was sold to cover the cost of the funeral, and since Anna had been kind to the deceased, she was asked whether she would like anything from the remaining bits and pieces. On my behalf, she chose three boxes in fine polished wood, among them this desk. The second box, next in size, was for jewellery and the third, the smallest, was the prettiest, a conch inlaid on its front, though its purpose is still unknown to me. These, too, had locks. On the former the lock was broken, to the latter the key was missing.

Inside the desk, were two hard-backed photographs, one of an open-mouthed baby on a bearskin, the other of a haughty-looking young boy with round spectacles posing in a very Victorian studio, his elbow on a carved arm-chair a monumental plinth beside him; two cards and a piece of thick cardboard, seemingly cut from a larger piece and picturing a painting of two playful dogs in front of a heavy curtain and what might be a barrel. The card had been touched up in biro to make parts of the picture clearer. The barrel, the spots on the dogs, and in the foreground, a cage with a small grey creature in it that the dogs were barking at. One card was a Christmas greeting, in spring colours, pale green with a lace edge, three birds singing on a shepherd's staff encircled by blue and pink petunias. There was no handwritten message, but inside, in gold was printed *A Message of Love.* The other card was speckled with age-spots. It had been a standard card from the School Board for London and printed handwriting flowed into the personal handwriting of the Head Teacher of the particular school awarding *This Card. This Card* was displayed in flamboyant Old English Text script in the centre. *P.* or *S. Chudwick,* Head Teacher of *Walnut Tree Walk School* had awarded this card to *Alice Gregory, a scholar in the IV Standard, for Punctual and Regular Attendance during the School Quarter ended June 31 1879.* There is a faded gold and blue frame around the text and at the top a medallion of a child's face over what might be a large collar or flower petals or even cherub-like wings. The bottom medallion was less clear. It looks like a grown-up angel handing something to a child. On looking closer, the angel's wing took on the shape of a scythe.

Little Alice Gregory was probably born in 1870 in London, or maybe in Somerset or Wiltshire from whence her surname comes. I can't remember her surname at the time we became her neighbours. Maybe because it was difficult to think she must have once married in order to have changed it. And she really was a little old lady, smaller then I was then at the age of ten, as if she had all her years remained a pupil in the IV Standard only outwardly growing older.

In 1870 in Italy, the "Third Rome", as it was called, was born. Rome had been the Rome of the Cæsars, the Rome of the popes and now was to be the Rome of the people, after being snatched back from the tug-of-war that had been going on for years between Austria and Prussia and France with the Vatican in the middle and Russia hanging around on the periphery. When the Treaty of Versailles was signed in the January of 1871, little Alice had begun to try out her first words, perhaps taken her first steps. She would have known nothing of these troubles abroad, nor that Britain wanted to be friends with Italy. Probably she never got to know about Italy's liberal movement or that Karl Marx was living just across the river from where she was punctually attending Walnut Tree Walk School, the trees long gone. All these countries, personified by contemporaries and historians alike, squabbling away like school-children of the kind she would have kept clear of in the playground, appear as giant monsters compared to her small person and would have kept her awake at night if she had known of their existence or how their squabbles and making-up was to affect her future.

When she started school she had already learned how to behave and would not dream of staying away from class or in any way making trouble. In spite of the fact that she did not always understand what was going on in the lessons, not only in History, but also in Geography and Mathematics. If she had been awarded a card in other subjects than punctuality and attendance, she would surely have kept them in her secret writing box and cherished them as remembrances of tidier times.

Little Alice must have been 82 when she died. Victoria was queen when she was born and Elizabeth II came to the throne the year she died.

During those intervening years, revolutions, wars, reforms, shaky times of peace, assassinations and an abdication occurred, inspiring enough books to fill several libraries of Alexandria, and as many more which now are lost. Histories, biographies, novels, poems, spy stories, archives of documents, articles, not to forget all the letters written leaning on diverse supports in the dug-outs, some unspeakable, other than a portable writing desk – all spewed out about The Great War and the Second World War and all that lay between. And all these events would have affected the life of Alice Gregory.

The fragile peace following the Treaty ending the first war was just a catching of breath before the second. In Britain, those at home did not see the horrors of the trenches, but they saw and felt the consequences for those who came back. In the second war, they saw the results down the road. Neighbouring houses were razed to the ground. Holes hollowed out of memory, nerve endings brutally cut over, shrivelled up, leaving synapses to fend for themselves as best they could. People needed all those books to fill the gaping holes they walked around with inside themselves as much as they needed the town-plans made to fill the yawning gaps surrounding them. To help them back to a world where people read books. Winston Churchill, the "war monger" as Anna and others with her called him, though not our neighbour I am sure, filled many of the holes to which he had contributed. His formidable *A History of the English-speaking Peoples* ends with the words: *The future is unknowable, but the past should give us hope.* Has it? Has the past given reason to hope? It would seem that we never cease to scratch surfaces eager to gather another piece of knowledge of the past, perhaps searching for a story, a history, an idea which will give us the hope we all sorely need.

And one of those *English-speaking peoples,* one English-speaking person, the little old lady, once known as Alice Gregory, what did *she* know? What were *her* hopes? Who came to her and filled a gap in her life, only to leave her with a new? She lived alone with her married name, and that, too, disappeared after her death, no longer remembered. But the certificate for good behaviour kept faithfully among the memorabilia of her past has ensured her a place in the thoughts of a stranger, - me.

In so many ways, Anna, my mother, contributed to my enjoyment over the written word. She gave me encouragement and freedom. Yet when faced with what she did not understand, she destroyed it.

At the time, as I grew more daring in my use of language and more coherent with the practice of it, my endeavours must have developed a certain authenticity as she would ask me at times about this person or that, as if I should know of whom she was speaking. I had never heard of these people, guessing that she must have confused the English names, not dreaming to connect these names with those of my fictional characters, and blissfully ignorant of the fact that my apparent lack of recognition when interrogated about these individuals and what they might mean to me, was to her a dissemblance of my guilt that gave her strong grounds for suspicion and even stronger grounds for her to protect me from myself.

I had committed a cardinal error when counting on the universal understanding of poetic license, or that the writer's 'I' could speak for another. This point is, I realize, debatable. Not, however, for mother. As she clandestinely but righteously read, the written 'I' was unequivocal. It was the voice of her daughter, recording her actions.

My writings revealed to her my loose moral condition. It was, thus, her duty as a mother to act for my best. I was in danger. The poisonous flower must be cut off in the bud. There was no need to discuss the matter with me, or with anyone else who might have pointed out that she was living in England where cutting poisonous buds out of children was not quite the done thing, whereas, as a point of interest, the administering of a well-deserved beating was quite acceptable. No. No discussion. She was, after all, a Roman, and as a Roman and the head of her family, had definite rights over her child. And as a Roman was ever cognizant of her duty.

So, one night – it must have been a night for such a deed – she destroyed page after page of the documentation of a young person's thoughts and fantasies, a personal project for future reference, a safeguard against the veil of comfortable forgetfulness, a point of reference for the one the writer wished to become.

I had had no illusions about my mother's righteous curiosity but, to my mind, if I succumbed to locking up my private papers, I had felt I would be condoning her behaviour. Instead, I willed her, wordlessly, to respect my right to privacy.

It was of course asking for trouble. To be honest, I had expected trouble. But not destruction.

Paradoxically, this situation, despite my overt display of fury, forced me, raging, into hiding. Full of righteous fury, I decided to go undercover. She was sure she had done what was right. There was no way in which I could shake her belief in that. But I could bide my time. I became a demon to myself.

Once upon a time, demons were not evil. They were deities, spirits, the spirit we all have in us, our *genius.* They were more akin to fairies. And this demon-fairy of mine did not emerge into the light of day for many, many years. For, as everyone knows, who knows fairies, before their spells can be broken, they must reveal themselves.

The Dark Fairy, the fairy-tale witch, the one who was not invited to the christening of Sleeping Beauty, is not perhaps the Bad Fairy her reputation suggests, but more the Fairy of Shadows. Everyone feared her, as they fear shadows. They were unable to see that her promise was in fact a true gift to the baby princess, who it would seem, had everything. The spell put her to sleep, and the same spell woke her up. This fairy is the spell-maker who compels us to find out for ourselves what is truly for our own good. She forces us to develop, to make use of the gifts the Good Fairies throw, effortlessly, into our cradles, and for which they receive unmitigated recognition.

One of my Good Fairies was the woman who bore me, unwillingly, into this world, and who disappeared shortly after my first christening, which was a provisional one, as is the tradition of Baptists, the faith of the large family to which she belonged. In that family there was no room for one more. It was not in the order of things that an unknown soldier, on leave from fighting the good fight, should find joy and release from horror and dread of death in a dance and a cuddle, ending up inside a tiddly virgin, still waiting for her own soldier boy who was away "Fighting abroad". Might not he, when home again from the horror of war, in compassion with a fellow fighter, perhaps having himself sought quick comfort before facing possible death, might not he have made room in his house for the earth-child of his dream-woman, loved it as his own, since it had been fathered in life's thrust to conquer death by another soldier just like himself?

And maybe, for a while, when she felt the stir of new life disturb her sleep, the betrothed herself sequestered the thought that she could keep her child, that she could tell him what had happened, as she told me a lifetime later, or she could dissemble the truth. Dissemblance would mean having to live with her secret forever. How could she bear that?

As it turned out, that is what she had to do.

My mother, the woman from Rome, came late, like the dark fairy she was, with the law on one side and the reluctant child-bearer on the other, snatched me from the cradle, staged a new christening, called a baptism among Catholics, to whose faith *she* adhered. Her dark-fairy nature stayed around in disguise to show up at critical moments, to comfort and to demand.

In truth it must be said that she was also a whole bundle of ordinary, everyday good fairies. These were often brought out on display. Perhaps too much harsh light of day caused their pretty colours to fade after a while. The one who was kept in the dark, however, is slowly emerging from the shadows, her features becoming more and more clear-cut. Penetrating her disguise has, nevertheless, been a shock, and took us both unawares. The feeling it left was like something tabu, slightly erotic, slightly perverse. The feeling a Victorian virgin might have had at the first sight of male genitals: having deduced there was something different about a man, but not in her wildest dreams had she imagined anything like that. It was a loss of innocence, yet incomplete. It was indeed like the prick of the needle that put the whole palace to sleep.

It was a premature coming-of-age. And it was a shock.

As my mother's own loss of innocence had been.

But first, she was born.

2

The thirty first of May, 1889, the day on which she was born, in Gallicano nel Lazio, a short distance from Rome, the weather was as lovely as it can get at that time of year, in that particular part of the world.

For over a week, high pressure had been building up over Central Europe, while low as usual over the British Isles with their eternal drizzle. In Rome that day the temperature was around 28 degrees Celsius. In Gallicano, higher above sea level than Rome, the winds would have been gentle and refreshing. The sky was cloudless. The last day of May held all the promises of an early hot Summer and a fruitful Autumn, a good sign for the grape-harvest.

A few days after her birth the baby was baptized as Paulina Anna Maria D'Offizi, and, for more than half of her life, was known by those who loved her as Nina. At twenty-six she married and changed her surname to Levi, whose tribal origins were not to be mistaken. Enrico Levi, from Mantova, violinist and medical doctor, younger than his bride, was an only son. In choosing a Gentile, a Catholic at that, he ended his family line, even if there had been children. Which there were not. He not only ended his branch of the tribal tree, he severed it, alienating himself from his mother and his sister, (I heard nothing of a father) both of whom his wife claimed hated her, which was probably true. She was a woman of great charm, with absolutely no inclination to ingratiate herself with those who disliked her, unless she had a good reason.

Young Enrico Levi had indeed been charmed by her, as many other men were, before him and after, until the end of her life. He adored her. I have her word for it. And she professed to have loved him, and would boast that there was no other man like him. Yet however great her love for him might have been, she was unable to overcome her horror of childbirth and bless him with a baby. What irony! However minuscule the amount of seed that might seep into her un-Jewish womb, the terrified Nina would rinse it out with religious thoroughness. According to one of her cautionary tales, her womb lay on the wrong side, necessitating an operation if she were to bear a child through gestation to birth. It was the operation that filled her with such fear, she said.

She had maybe forgotten the terror that had overcome her when a grown man had exposed himself to her, a carefree child, dancing her make-believe dance in the woods, the sunny woods full of birdsong, close to her home, her fortressed village in Lazio where she was safe and happy and sang like a bird herself all day long.

Could it have been guilt, or some other more obscure sin, she later sought to expiate, many years later, long after dr. Levi's untimely death from pneumonia after a careless summer chill, (Had she not pleaded with him to guard himself against the treacherous evening damp?), when well past the child-bearing age, she decided it was the right thing to do, in the War's dearth of fathers and overabundance of motherless children, to take one of these discarded creatures to her breast. A girl, of course.

The war in question here is the Second World War, so-called, as I, too, must call it, being myself part of the little world of European omnipotence, or impotence, that still refused to accept the discoveries of new worlds after nearly five hundred years. Anna had been in other wars. She had been a volunteer nurse in Italy's attack on North Africa, had seen its barbaric consequences, and was returned home with shell-shock, and with the life-long image of a beach filled with flying limbs and dismembered bodies. After the impact of the bomb, she looked up into the face of a German officer. She could not utter a word. For three months. She recovered from the shock but not from that memory.

Mussolini was on the rise and she could see what kind of a star he was. She was the widow of a Jew. She was taking no chances. She was not the wait-and-see type. She had to leave Italy.

Leaving Italy cannot have been an easy decision for her to make. Yet I don't remember her ever bewailing the decision itself. What I remember is how she looked back with longing to the country in which she had grown up and in which she had already lived a life, surrounded by her loved ones and an abundance of everything else she loved, fruit ripened on the tree, wine, bread baked in stone-ovens, olive oil, fresh cheese, home-made pasta, a myriad of foodstuffs that post-war Britain had scarcely heard of, and grapes, not least grapes hanging from the vine. Most of all she missed the sun. The hot and golden sun, from which you could seek shelter under the trellis and vine-leaves of a pergola, the ideal spot for the enjoyment of the everyday delicacies of country life, not the pale, moon-like representation that shone over England, if it had the strength to show itself at all. She should have been forewarned, with all her interest for all things English, not least her reading, which told her that in London the death of the sun had been mourned a century ago. As if fiction was not quite to be believed.

There is a photograph of her taken after her return to her native land, twenty-five years after her leaving, sitting on a makeshift chair under such a pergola, a bucket full of peaches and pears kept cool in water at her side, at a table laid for a lunchtime break at one end of a vineyard. *Her* vineyard. You can feel the heat of the sun in the sharp contrast the motley shadows of the slightly moving vine-leaves made on the faces. Those sitting with her around the table were smiling. She was not smiling. She was looking proudly into the eye of the camera.

She was a proud woman. In many meanings of the word. Before the war, the same war she had tried to avoid, she was proud of her grapes and the wine that came from them. As soon as she had settled in England, she imported a cellar-full of this wine. She needed her liquid sunshine in order to exist among the grey streets of London. If the city was not paved with gold, she could at least bury her own gold under it. She found a fellow Italian with a shop and a storing cellar and hoarded her treasure there.

Wine. Her treasure. Her inheritance. For the Sufi of Arabia, wine is the symbol of wisdom, of mysterious inspiration, of spiritual love.

For Anna, it was the embodiment of life itself.

"The one who does not like wine," she would say, as she drank a draught of the deep red liquid from Algeria, labelled simply 'Algerian Wine', and acknowledged at the opening of each bottle as 'cheap but good', "the one who does not like wine, let him be denied a glass of water."

She had a dramatic turn of phrase. The truth was that if she were to hear anyone cry out in need of a glass of water, she would be the first to run and fetch it. As Mrs. Shorr, for instance.

Mrs. Shorr was another little old lady whose path crossed Anna's path. Or rather, Mrs. Shorr was stationary if not standing still, that would not have been her, and Anna came along and crossed hers.

She was for several years our landlady. She owned and lived in a detached house in South West London, and rented out two rooms on the first floor with use of bathroom. When I was in my teens, the last of my mother's projects to earn money, quickly and a lot of it, had failed, so that to play it – life, I presume, - more safely we came to live in rented rooms. Once more, Anna had to live at the grace of others.

An English detached house with a living-in landlady was not very detached on the inside. It was a three-bedroomed house, and to all outward appearances very like the house-of-our-own I had imagined. Mrs. Shorr slept in the master-bedroom, still so called although for 30 odd years at least its mistress had ruled there alone, mostly awake. Anna and daughter occupied the other two bedrooms. There was a tiny bathroom with enough room for one at the sink, or for two if the other soaked in the bath-tub. Later, we were four to share these amenities.

Mrs. Gould moved in as Mrs. Shorr's companion, though she paid rent as we did. The 'companion' title clearly distinguished her from us, the Italian and her polite English daughter. Mrs. Gould was quite English, well-spoken and large in an English country way, as if used to both horses and garden parties. She believed it was comme- il-faut to extend her little finger when holding her tea-cup. She had one other advantage in this household: she too was Jewish, like Mrs. Shorr.

Mrs. Shorr was in no way English. She had no pretenses to genteel manners, if she knew at all what they might be, not that she was rough or directly impolite. Hers was rather the frightened response of a country simpleton, who was clinging to the meagre habits of childhood in the complexities of adult life in a metropolis. She was a Russian who had fled Russia with her husband around the time of the first revolutionary outbreak. Judging from the scratched photograph on her dust-free dressing table in the master-now-mistress bedroom, she could not have been more than sixteen or seventeen at the time of their wedding. He was slightly older and looked directly into the camera with an air of seriousness and responsibility about him, his head tilted forward. She was looking into nowhere. Her eyes were pale and watery, her mouth was set like that of a child who wonders what is going on, her lips not quite together, the lower lip hanging as if forgotten, making her seem dazed. She was neither pretty nor plain. As yet unformed, inane. A look she never lost, though it became desiccated and dark.

According to Mrs. Gould, her companion, Mrs. Shorr was an analphabetic, which information made certain quirks in her behaviour more understandable. For instance, when she hurried to the dark kitchen-dresser in her scullery whenever asked to sign for something, a recommended letter or lottery tickets from the local school. She had to have her glasses, she would say, but there were no other glasses there apart from the ones on her nose. And then there were the times when she would emerge from the kitchen suddenly into the hall if she heard someone descending or ascending the stairs, given away by the creak. There is always one stair that creaks on a staircase, though this one was muffled by carpeting. She popped up, propelled out of her safe-place behind the scullery shadows, in order to speak of the news which she had just culled from the newspaper she held in her hand. Only her version was often quite a different one from the one in print. Mostly not only was her version different but the news itself was different. She would construe a drama or scandal from photos and isolated words. Maybe she had learnt to read and write as a child. In cyrillic.

How frightening and confusing it must have been for her to be married off, sent off to a strange country where she understood nothing, not even the shape of the letters of the alphabet.

She remained frightened and confused over the years. If things – such things as a dispute with Anna, with long training in winning disputes whoever was in the right – got too complicated for her, she would begin to scream, a high-pitched penetrating scream that merited the expression *blue murder*. That type of screaming brings an end to any dispute.

The coming of Mrs. Gould brought a certain harmony and English sensibility into the household, doubling the diplomatic corps of one in the effort to keep an armistice between the illiterate Russian Jew, exiled against her inclination and the anarchistic Catholic from an ancient Italian family.

Ironically, Mrs. Shorr never knew that the love of Anna's life had been a Jew.

Mrs. Gould moved into the front sitting-room with its charming bay-window, with a view of the lawn and lilacs and of the road. Our rooms upstairs looked out on the back garden where the *pièce-de-resistance* was an old pear tree that flowered in spite of its age in an astonishing Biblical fashion every spring.

There was also a view of the Grammar school, as it was then called, consisting of two spacious Victorian houses, one of which had been the home of the comedian Dan Leno, laid back from the road, protected with iron railings, joined together by a later building in yellow brick which housed the chapel and the nun's quarters. "La Retraite" was, as its name suggests, a place for retreats from the bustle and strife of daily life. It had kept its name and in part its function even though the nuns had become a teaching order. Not in view from the road, nor from the upper bed-rooms in Mrs.'s Shorr's establishment, were the wonderful gardens and playing fields. The hockey pitch was for ladies' hockey, a most un-ladylike game believed to foster action and team spirit. These gardens were in themselves a retreat. An unreal world as unreal as the Shorr residence.

One of the two bedrooms served as a living-room, meaning that was where 'living' took place. In one shadowy corner was the kitchen, a tiny stove and a light blue dresser in the new wonder material - Formica.

In front of the window, the pear-tree window, was the dining-cum-writing table, where Anna did her pools every week or studied form for her modest but successful betting on horses. The remaining space in the middle of the room in front of the fire-place was the sitting-room, defined by a small sofa. In the opposite corner to the kitchen, was Anna's armchair, halfway into the dining area. Here, she could keep an eye on her diminished domain. Or she might doze off, while her daughter spread herself on the not very large sofa, yet large enough for her to sit or lie in various possible positions, decorous or indecorous, while balancing a book on her chest. Anna read as well, classics and newspapers. She deemed it beneath her morals to read the News of the World but bought it for the crossword, which was easier than that of *The Sunday Times* or *The Observer*, especially for a non-native speaker.

If on looking up from her paper, or mending, she saw her daughter reclining with her reading, with her legs splayed out over the back of the sofa, she would reprimand her on her shameless revealing of bare skin and underwear.

"But there's only you and me here! And you've seen it all before!"

"Never mind that! It's a bad habit. You might forget when you are somewhere else, with strangers."

"It's different at home,"

"*Stai composta!*"

Resorting to Italian was her way of putting an end to the discussion. The truce was conceded by pulling a skirt or a blanket over the knees, thus restoring decency.

Perhaps it was her own fear of her daughter flaunting her nakedness in strange company that she wanted to cover up.

Although Mrs. Shorr was the definite and rightful owner of this small corner mansion perfectly positioned for anyone interested in the comings and goings in a quiet residential cross-roads in the suburbs, whoever rang the front-door bell would have taken her for an ancient and faithful maid.

Her uniform was the perennial English flowery wrap-around pinafore with piping in the colour of one of its flowers, accompanied by lisle stockings and carpet slippers. Her girlish figure had stiffened over the years and the adult-sized garment was more like a frivolous winding-sheet that kept her upright. She was very thin so her legs could not fill her stockings, which hung in loose folds above her slippers, a classic brown and beige check felt with a shiny brown pom-pom in front, until it fell off after many years of use, leaving a few loose threads as a reminder.

She would be constantly, but slowly, moving all day long, washing, dusting, polishing, hoovering, hovering, sneaking around in her silent slippers. She weighed so little that the creaky step near the top of the staircase hardly sighed when she trod on it. If one of her lodgers came home, she would hear her immediately and her head would pop up from behind some door or other, brown and grey as if in a Punch and Judy show for the aged, where all the bright colours are removed and grown dark.

If by chance a stranger, a salesman, someone making inquiries, should come to her dustless doorstep and ring the doorbell, they would, and often did, take her for the housekeeper from her dress and from her frightened and challenging look.

"Good morning, madam. May I speak to the lady of the house?"

"Yes," she would answer, not moving a muscle or widening the slit of the open door and stretching the 'e' in 'yes' to 'ye-es'.

"Would you mind calling her for me?"

"Yes". Still no movement, not of face nor of door. Only a stretched out vowel.

The still-stand might end with:

"We don't want anything. You must speak to Mrs. Gould."

And before the door finally shut:

"Maybe I could speak to her...?"

"Mrs. Gould is not here."

"When will she...?"

As the door closes, in a shrill fearful cry:

"She is not here!"

The thin scream hung on the closed door.

The bottles of Algerian red, along with the fat-bellied bottles of Australian burgundy for special occasions, were purchased in Soho, at an off-license near Greek street. It was a tall narrow building, squeezed in between two larger establishments which gave it an old-fashioned look. The owner was a fellow Italian, her friend from before the war, and to whom, Anna, in fear of the bombing more for her fortune than for her life, had sold her entire holding of wine, 'cheap'.

One night, after a bout of bombing, the shops nearby lay in ruins. Needless to say, the cellar remained intact. Not a single bottle of her wine was even cracked, as she would say. The buyer did well and the balance of friendship changed.

Anna used to go there as to a local shop, sometimes with me in tow, to be shown off as a better investment perhaps. She would buy her parmesan or panettone as if in Italy, bestowing her favours as a customer. Wine was another matter. On that point, she was still in spirit a proprietor.

The erstwhile friend and his wife smiled their welcome with the appropriate gestures, but their smiles did not quite reach their eyes, and their '*buongiornos*' had an empty echo.

"*Come sta, signora*" held a similar double sound. Was she come to claim, or did she expect to be honoured?

The shop was clearly prospering, while the shop-owners complained of the difficult times, as shop-owners will. She was convinced that her pre-war store of most excellent wine had made the shop-keeper's fortune.

Anna, of course, expected gratitude.

Gratitude for what to her mind were her good deeds, was the greatest of all her expectations in her life, also the most devastating. Her expectancy of gratitude as the natural order of things brought her greatest disappointments.

Since she was convinced that her pre-war store had made the shop-keeper's fortune, his acknowledgement of her influence would have brought her some good fortune in turn, she believed. No such acknowledgement was forthcoming, so she turned to another source. One she could rely on not to fail her, since he was long dead and buried. She turned to Napoleon. Not to his life and times, though she admired him, as an Italian, and gave her daughter his empress' name, which more by chance than choice happened also to be the name of Anna's own grandmother. Nor did she turn to his life which reflected, you might say, both great fortune and great *mis*fortune, ending in exile as hers also ended, but to his guiding thoughts as how to deal with life, as laid down in his *Book of Fate.*

This book, in the pink, of all colours, hard-backed English version, had accompanied her from place to place all the years I knew her.

Together with the *Book of Fate*, there was always a second book, a loose-leaved affair with brittle brown pages in Italian, almost not a real book, only the remains of one. The pages were filled with drawings of different faces placed each one next to a different animal head. Face and animal head were paired according to likeness, so you did not have to be able to read Italian, or read at all, to understand the method of categorization used. They were plain look-alikes. Round eyes and a small pursed mouth was put next to an owl. Sharp pointed nose and eyes close together was next to a fox. A large-beaked nose and heavy-lidded eyes, next to an eagle. And so on, duck, hen, pig, horse, lion and mouse. And so on. All illustrating the appropriate characteristics of human diversity. I used to use a card to cover the one picture so as to guess what its pair would be. I also tried to glean some information on the personalities connected with each type from the Italian text. But this guesswork ended inevitably in frustration.

Frustration and language were paired words as far as my mother was concerned. Not a paragon of patience at the best of times, a facet of her personality of which she usually prided herself, when it came to translating it had to be simultaneous. She would not tolerate the slightest hesitation in the flow of sound. A word in one language, Italian for instance, which did not recall instantly the same word in English, invariably provoked a stream of invectives, which were always in Italian, and gave an impression of Italian life and discourse to which she otherwise seldom alluded.

The contents of these two books alone would have supported the proposition that character is destiny.

There was, however, a third item in Anna's travelling trunk: a pack of cards.

It must be remembered that Anna was a practical woman, not a mystic or fairground fortune-teller. Understanding human nature and fate with the aid of great men of history were necessary basics, but not enough in order to survive in this difficult world. She needed to be a step ahead. She had to know what human nature was up to, and what fate had in store.

Among the loosely held leaves of the book on human character, albeit in animal forms, was a section on palmistry, now with drawings of human hands. Here you could get an idea of how many children, or marriages, if any, you could expect, and, roughly, how long you would live.

The cards could do more than that. They could give you a detailed look into your future life. They were not ordinary cards, although they had once been part of the pack with which we are all familiar when playing Bridge or Piggy, or Poker. These cards, however, were all picture cards, symbols or personifications. They had an aura of age. One side was patterned vaguely in a misty brown. The other, the picture side, was in hauntingly beautiful colours, with a creamy band under each representation to give room for its mysterious title.

Hidden books and unknown cards have a particular fascination for any child. For me, their fascination was increased by the fact that my mother disliked me handling her cards or poking my nose into any of her personal effects. A clandestine feeling was woven into my curiosity, and I could play with those picture cards for hours if, on occasion, I found myself alone at home. Years later, I discovered that what I had been playing with was a Tarot pack. The tool of the fortune-teller, indeed.

No one knows for sure the origins of the Tarot cards. The Sufis claim them as theirs, and indeed a game of cards was brought from the Saracens to Viterbo in 1379, at least according to the Italian chronicler, Feliciano Busi.

For the Sufis, the images were a method for storing their wine, their particular wine, that "existed before what you call the grape and the vine".

Unaware, almost certainly, of the Moorish origins of her pack of cards, she carried, none the less, in her the righteous harshness of the Moors, their contribution to the Spanish Inquisition. She was a carrier. The virus was in her blood.

I was not blood of her blood. Yet some form of contagion must have made the leap from her to me.

The latency period was long but the disease was there, and broke out as it must. I finally recognized all the signs: disdain, repugnance, hatred, and the most insufferable of all the shades of rage, contempt, Anna's contempt of the mean, the puny, the pusillanimous. I have watched the way she crushed a flea between her thumbnails. I have seen her with disgust on her face incarcerate a toad in a drainpipe. I cannot do the like. Swatting a gnat gives me nausea. Even so, I carried her disease.

And something else, some undefinable else. In another vein, I carried what must have emerged from an unknown twist in the genetic spiral. A twist that neither she nor I knew anything about. A vein parallel to the artery that bore deep-drunk, wine-kindled blood coursing in my body. A parallel vein, a vein of gold-ore in the dark earth-rock, reflecting the ruby-red of the wine we drank together, to the toast of her Bacchic curse. This other vein that proved to have absorbed that other wine, the wine of the Sufis, the wine of wisdom that had existed before the grape and the vine, and which nourished the eye of the Seeker. In each our own way, we carried those drops, too.

After I reached and passed the age of reason, we quarrelled. Always. Year after year, I opposed her every belief, opinion, turn of phrase. Far beyond the natural introversion of puberty and the belligerent assertiveness of youth.

It was a question of survival. Her or me.

The struggle ended when she died. Outwardly.

In his *Book of Knowledge* the philosopher El-ghazali writes that "people oppose things because they are ignorant of them."

Was that *my* opposition?

My ignorance?

Of who she really was?

I oppose her no longer, that I can truly say, speaking from a dark place deep in my heart.

Yet I must ask myself: do I now know her?

Know her enough to say this is love?

3

It takes a wise man to know his own child, the saying goes. And I like to think that Eleonoro D'Offizi was a wise man. His daughter thought so. She adored him. She loved her mother, but she adored her father. Her mother died early, contracting peritonitis after the birth of her youngest child, a boy, who did not live long himself. Nina was nine when her mother died, thus becoming the older of the two surviving children of her father's second marriage. There were several older children, but they were dismissed in my mother's tale of her early life as vehicles of envy and jealousy. They too had lost a mother once, and then a step-mother, and must necessarily have been touched by their double loss however ambivalent their feelings towards their half-sister may have been. As Anna saw it, they were against her, the daughter who enjoyed the father's acclaim. He, in sorrow after his wife's death, could not have been a just go-between among his children. His beloved Nina would have taken the lead, full of righteousness in action. Someone had to take their mother's place, and she, of course, was not one to be caught up in mean jealousy. Her father loved her most, so that was that. The vacancy was hers to fill. And, as it was and would continue to be, he relied on her completely. Nina had already at that early age complete confidence in her inherent capabilities, not without grounds as it proved. In spite of that fact, to the casual observer it seemed a heavy burden to carry for such a young girl.

The older children, almost grown up, appeared in her tales as shadowy greedy shapes, who made life difficult for her father, and for her, his favourite, and who together with him was, after all, doing her best for the youngest daughter, Rosa. Rosa perhaps did not quite realize that she had lost her mother, so well did Nina step into the shoes of caretaker and decision-maker, while father was on his travels, and maybe even when he was not. There was a nanny, of course, who had been there for many many years, and whom Nina, bountiful more than sharing, considered her own. So, with the usual maelstroms of envy, jealousy, sorrow, longing, mourning, competition and adoring love, Nina grew up and grew strong on family life.

In 1870, when Italy finally became Italy, united one might say in its Italian way, Eleonoro D'Offizi must have been a fine young man getting on for thirty. He would then have grown to manhood during the troubled '60s, and was probably born at the beginning of the '40s, starting his life as a school-boy when upheaval and revolution touched all of Europe. The English version of these European changes came more quietly, with Parliamentary discussions, dissent and reforms. However, political discussions in England could be as vociferous as in Italy when roused, and one of the voices there crying out for reform was Charles Dickens, the favourite-writer-to-be of a girl yet unborn. Under the birds-eye-view of time distant paths may be seen to cross. Nina's father may well have managed to be born during the time when Dickens visited Italy, or the 'almost Italy' of 1844. Maybe the young Count di Cavour, though a disbeliever in the pragmatics of Italy's unification, an ardent advocate of freedom and for reform of absolutism, might also, in his many travels to the England he admired, have been familiar with Dickens, writer and public figure. Just as Eleonoro's father may well have been born about the same time as Garibaldi began school, if *he* had had time for school. According to Anna, her grandmother never forgave Garibaldi for the injuries her husband received when accompanying the general as his secretary.

Do generals at war have secretaries, I used to wonder.

Anna always served her facts with such aplomb and represented with such sensitivity the feelings of those involved, using her scenic talent to the full on the limited audience of one, though anyone who heard her would feel transported backstage in a privileged performance of the drama of the history of Italy, played by one of those who had been there. Whether or not anyone she knew really had been there has in the course of the years become an academic question. She had most certainly been there in her fashion, which was a most exciting one and fired, literally, my childish imagination, yet was unable to extinguish the fire of the other flame bred in me, that of the prim English sceptic. I told this tale only to the trusted few, those who knew my mother and therefore with a tasty pinch of salt could believe it and enjoy.

She came from an old family, which could trace its ancestors back to before the fifteenth century. She did not talk about them much. What was there to say, she had never met them, they were simply facts, and there were no doubts about her claims in this area. A beautiful document where the family name was displayed on a painted coat of arms, under which prominent members of the family were mentioned in a handwritten account, lay rolled up in her trunk along with her books. The shield was decorated with three diagonal red bands, crossed by one band in blue with three golden stars. At the top and sides of the shield was the framework in silver of a coat of armour, and topping the whole emblem was a gold crown embellished with red painted drapes. The inscription tells that the family originates from Milan, and from there moved to Liguria, so to Lazio then to Umbria. In the fifteenth century,

Guiseppe was feudal king of Busuago and Roncello, Giorgio was colonel in the Imperial Army stationed in Prague, and that his son was captain at the court of Vienna. Further, it mentions Andrea, distinguished doctor and philosopher, Girolamo a judge, Valentino an architect, and Luigi cardinal and chancellor of the Holy Roman Church and Apostolic delegate. The final mention is of Ubaldo from Viterbo in 1700.

Did Ubaldo play cards, I wonder?

There is a gap of a hundred years before Anna's story picks up a thread crossing the tapestry of Time, as her grandfather's appearance on the scene touches that of Garibaldi, who was born in 1807. *In a hundred years, all is forgotten,* they say. But that is not necessarily so. Not if there are connections, weaving a familiar pattern, where there is yearning, a pressing need to remember the past, when the future is uncertain, and the present is disappointing.

What did Eleonoro remember of his childhood, of his mother's bitterness towards Italy's hero and the difficult task of unifying such divergent states? Was that the reason why he allowed himself to be caught up with the times, when Italy became enamoured of all things English, and the English enamoured of Italy itself? When the inebriating extract from the grape and the vine attracted English poets more than the poetry produced from Sufic wisdom? Was there already strife in his personal life, that made animals appeal to him more than people, and horses most of all? He became a travelling salesman of race-horses, and sold to the English Royalty. His daughter sometimes accompanied him and herself fell in love with all things English. She became enamoured in the way Titania becomes enamoured of Bottom in his disguise as a donkey, which turned out to be no disguise but a true transformation. What word other than "enamoured" can I use for this state resembling love that is not love but an outward shine, hard like enamel and cracking under a hard blow?

Anna was already enchanted with her father's enchantment, and the England she saw fascinated her. She would recall vividly her fascination long after the outer veils had been removed.

"All those little houses, I said to my father, they are like dolls-houses. Oh, how I would love to live in a little house like that. I would be so happy. And he laughed."

Her voice would invoke the surprise and joy of a young girl whose father adores her and will grant her every wish, in that long ago, before she learnt to be wary of wishing.

Then her voice would change. Imbued with the patina of the years in between, it darkened and hardened. Her desire and expectation had turned into regret and disappointment.

"Ah," she would sigh, "my poor father. If he could see me now."

In that "now" lay all the insults thrown at the "bloody foreigner", all the rejections on the doorstep with "No children," because children were not wanted though dogs were allowed in those dolls-houses. No children meant no mothers as well. She who had sought to do some good in this war-ravaged country, taking to her heart one of their accidents of war, was sent packing on the threshold, with her shameful bundle, as if she herself had indeed suffered the joy and the pain of the baby's birth. If that baby had been unwanted at birth, how much more unwanted Anna must have felt on its behalf and on her own at each closing front-door, of each charming cottage or as time progressed all the less charming lodgings.

"Poor father." As if her disillusionment with the charms of England, once to her a perfect country in miniature, a play-world, where no one could be other than delightfully happy, as if *her* disillusionment were his. By comforting him, her poor father, she brought him to her, making him share with her bitter future. In so doing, she was not a woman completely without a man's protection. She felt she had a man who loved her and thus understood her plight. And so, in some small measure, she comforted herself.

Her daughter, at other times part of the great disappointment, was in moments like these a necessary listener, an essential part of Anna's inner monologue. Without a daughter, the loneliness of time passing would have been invisible. Would it have been less tolerable? I would like to think so.

Anna never stopped feeling the loss of her father. He died when she was sixteen.

"He died with his head on my arm. Right here," she would say, pointing to her right arm, and I would see his head resting there, as if in sleep, and felt embarrassed in my lack of experience, at being brought in to the room of a dying man and his grieving daughter.

I, too, still feel her loss, her loss of her father which I understand better with age, and my loss of her.

I cannot point to my arm, to draw her closer to me.

She died without me, with no arm to hold her. Maybe the quiet priest who had become her friend held her hand. He was the last man to succumb to her charms. He must have truly understood her desire to do good, to do what was right, according to God and to her own sense of justice. In this she steadfastly believed. This is what she meant when she would claim "I have my faith. Nothing can change that." She called it Catholicism. It was her own brand of Protestantism. She was as Catholic as Luther, or Henry VIII, or a Puritan with the trappings of the Roman ritual. She was a law unto herself. No pair of Mormon proselytes knocking on our London door in their funereal suits hanging uneasily large on their youthful shoulders, could get past her "No, thank you. I have my religion." And, if by chance she might take pity on them, as well she might, as she saw them standing there in the damp English weather, with their vulnerable faces and thin necks, and invited them in for a cup of tea, this admirable English habit she had picked up in her native land, they would have great trouble in getting in a word edgeways about the beliefs they had been sent out to preach, and would invariably melt, reluctantly at first, each with an eye to the other, and begin to enjoy their tea and biscuits, gradually absorbing a little of the loving care of one whose mind would not be changed.

The soft-spoken Catholic priest, a familiar figure in another foreign country, an even colder North, where her father had never been, visited her and enjoyed her company. A priest is also a father. For her, for whom the name 'father' meant so much, whereby in the wilderness of strangers she could cry out, as a Roman encouraged by Paul, she could cry out "Father". Priest. *Pater.* Father. *Papa. Babbino mio.* It was right and just that a father should hold her hand at the end. He said she had died peacefully, half in sleep.

Death.

Is it possible to understand what it is?

As a child, Anna had tried, as children do, to fathom the mystery of death and time passing.

"Daddy, will *I* die?"

"No, my darling. You will never die."

In the best of her worlds, it was the best of answers. She was consoled and the mystery remained untouched. Her father knew this once death could wait.

Anna's secret passion was Turkish Delight. The kind that came in small round plywood boxes, with exotic labels, that opened to reveal waxed paper folded like a whirling skirt. Under the folds were tightly packed fat cubes of pale glutinous jelly, generously covered with icing sugar.

The first box she had ever received had been a gift from her father. Where had he been to bring back such a gift for his young daughter? "Sweets to the sweet!" She would throw herself into his wide open arms. He would hold her tightly and swing her round as if she were still a child. He would taste her powdered cheek and smell the clean black of her hair. "Amore! Amore!" "Babbo mio!"

Is that what it had been like? As happy, as close? As sweet and as sticky? As ambiguous?

Far into old-age my mother was proud of her perfect teeth. At a time when the National Health system of Great Britain still existed and was moving into dentistry, and when the panacea for dental ailments was a relatively quick and painful prophylactic removal of the lot and the gift of state dentures, she had all reason to be proud when going on for seventy she could say: "They are all my own". Not one of these perfect teeth was a sweet one. Nevertheless, the mere sight of a small round plywood box of Turkish Delight would bring her close to a girlish swoon. Even allowing for her histrionic style, anyone could sense the underlying authenticity.

She must have been a Turkish delight herself in those golden days of her youth, with her perfect skin, pale and pink like those exquisite sweets, her pure-black hair enhancing the effect, like a precious ebony bowl. She knew how to heighten the paleness with silk face-powder on special occasions, and did so long after the baby plumpness of her cheeks had sunken to reveal the delicate structure of the bones, and the skin had softened into a myriad of imperceptibly fine lines. The light perfume of her powder remains with me to this day. *Yardley* it was called and there was a small round label featuring a languishing young lady in a pale pink crinoline. There was the air of an invisible English garden about her and all was reflected in those dusty grains of scent surrounding my mother. Her father must have loved that perfume as much as I did.

4

When did I first get to know her?

Does a baby *know* someone, in its nuzzling and nosing, sucking and sighing, in its vice-like clamping on breast or cheek, its clawing in contentment like a kitten, and like a kitten quite unaware of the pain it causes, or the pleasure? It knows the smell and the skin of the flesh it was recently a part of, that it was forced out of in turmoil and devastation. An extraordinary experience, never to be repeated thus never to be fully understood, and immediately relegated to the realms of forgetfulness. Then, nothing, only screaming. And then, once more, after an eternity, reunited with this body that was recently its own. Except it is no longer its own. The texture is different. The smoothness has a resistance in it, a dryness, contained in a new nothingness which is not nothingness but the air. It holds and it gives way. It changes from warm to cool, even cold, then hot again, dampens turns to fluid, as it was before. It is strange yet familiar. The taste is good. The mist on the skin smells like the taste. This is a good place just to be. How could this paradisal state fall into forgetfulness, with no vestige of the delight and the dread by which the dynasty ruled, except in the imagination.

How can anyone want to leave this Paradise?

Anna was always expressing herself in extremes. Which her daughter was forced to counteract from an early age. Or both mother and daughter would have tipped over into some dark void.

"My darling. How much do you love Mummy?" she might say, light as an afterthought, as it were.

This is no simple question in the general way of things, this question about the measuring of love, in itself a concept about which there is much feeling and some thought and definitely nothing of a conclusive nature. But to a three-year-old who has only just begun to understand the essence of measures, and can see with her little eye that long thin bottles of orange-juice have more in them than short fat ones, to her the question is simple, and yet even at that tender age she could hear the undertones throbbing in all their complexity.

Thinking back to the question and the space the answer opened around her like a swollen bubble, I can taste today the tart concentrate of post-war orange juice, with which the authorities intended to create a generation of healthy youth. I loved the taste and drank it preferably straight from its tall thin bottle, which meant that it never lasted until the next allotted ration.

Mummy was waiting.

"Lots," the child would answer, throwing her small arms around her mother's neck.

She was playing for time, the time needed to grow up out of her short plump body and have more to think with.

Mother's cradling arms were holding her back. An answer to the big question was wanted *now.*

"Come on, my darling. Tell Mummy how much you love her."

No longer a question, but a demand.

The three-year-old had to think quickly in the little round body she had, or she would never escape the cradling arms, and grow tall and thin. She thought hard, and images from her meagre experience of life and literature rose to help her.

"Three sacks!" she exclaimed, triumphantly.

Before her towered a shape, sudden as a shadow in oblique spotlight. She saw the sack of potatoes in the corner of the kitchen. It was huge. She could not believe they would ever eat up a whole sack of potatoes in their entire lifetimes. And she was constantly afraid it would topple over, and that the potatoes would roll out everywhere, and would disappear into murky kitchen corners and then there would be only a dirty sack lying there, empty. But one potato might hop out first and hit her in the eye and it would be her fault the other potatoes got away, because she wouldn't be able to see where they had rolled, and no one would be able to find them before they had begun to rot. But she was not thinking of that now. She must answer the question.

Three sacks was an enormous amount. There were always threes of everything in fairy-tales and there everything went on for ever.

"Three sacks!" she heard her mother repeat.

For one moment she was afraid that she had given the wrong answer.

Anna was overjoyed.

At least when she had clarified the true state of things, that is as to whether anyone else was valued at a three-sack price or more.

So even as this short dimpled body was bursting with love for this mother, faithful worshipper of weights and measures, it knew already that it would not do to burst with three sacks of potato love for anyone else.

And what if that small body really had burst, open, with that uncontainable feeling we call love? Or perhaps it did burst. Perhaps our bodies do, if only we had eyes left to see the flash, or ears to hear the thunder. The body surrounds the soul like the skin of a snake, a mortal coil shuffled off in the end, leaving – what? What becomes of the will, the wanting, the lusty joy? Where is it all? Is it hiding in those folds of flesh, or is every invisible want finally released?

Minute frogs sheltering under stones in a shady pool never explode into royalty. Distressed damsels wait dryly on the river-banks, fading in clouds of face powder into dusty specks.

What was it about, that dainty tale?

A tale of unrequited love to be forever read by lachrymose eyes, still clinging to their sockets of bone?

Is it possible to see, then, what is there? Without the passage of time that is the journey of the eye's perception to the point in the brain where understanding may be reached?

A frog is, after all, simply a frog.

A child is quite a different matter.

Do we ever completely slough that childhood-skin?

In becoming "Anna", that is what Nina did.

She threw off her old life. She changed her name, just as, when the time came, she changed mine.

When she made her journey to England in 1936 she was leaving a much-loved country that was showing signs of a madness she had not seen before.

As a young woman after the troubles in North Africa she saw the changes that had to come in the near-feudal system of which her family were a part, and imparted her radical views to her father. They must relinquish land to those who had fought for Italy before it was expropriated from them. Her father did not quite see the situation in that way. Which saddened her but did not stop her propagating what she thought right and practical, while bearing in mind what was bound to come about.

Whatever her bold action was, and of this no clear account was ever forthcoming, it resulted in Nina spending four nights hiding from the police in a cellar. Until it proved she had committed no crime, and was, as she had claimed, once more, right.

Authority had never daunted her. This early brush with politics, which demonstrated to her disbelief and amazement that speaking your mind, your right mind, to the powers above you was not sufficient to procure justice, left her with a distaste for anything political. And perhaps prepared her for an understanding of the forces behind Mussolini, propelling her once again into action, this time to save her own skin.

She was close to fifty when she made her last journey to England on an Italian passport. The passport cost her the earth. Her earth. She had perhaps considered the possibility, but she could in no way know for sure, that she was relinquishing the soil of her ancestors, the soil that kissed by the sun proliferated her sun-drenched wine, and which she drank with religious ecstasy. Like a sacrament. Believe me. And was maybe the only ecstasy she experienced. Apart from the opera. But I am being presumptuous. For what can we know of another's transfiguring passion when we are not present?

The passport also cost her a lot of money. With her Jewish husband's surname, obtaining a passport was no routine matter. She had to bribe the chief-of-police, a "good friend" as fortune would have it, who supplied her with a so-called private passport. This meant it was only valid for three months, presumably to ensure the return of citizens for possible internment.

Paulina Anna D'Offizi, married Levi, prepared for a longer journey than would have been apparent to the border officials. They could not have been aware that they had met more than their match in determination and subterfuge.

How could they have guessed that the lovely widow seeking solace among friends in England, a country she had visited many times since her youth, that this superficial, rich young woman with contacts among English Royalty, as she made sure to inform them, had thousands of lire sewn into her elegant clothes, and long strings of natural pearls hidden in the violin case of her husband's violin, from which she could never be parted, and which in itself was worth enough to keep her alive for a considerable time. How could they know that the ring on her finger and those in her ears were real diamonds, family heirlooms her husband had given her on their wedding day? How could they know that they were allowing a small fortune to pass out of Italy, or that the heart of the woman before them was full of fear, fear of being held back more than fear of the unknown? A fear subdued with the sorrow of having to leave her true fortune - her land, her vineyards, her family, her sister Rosa, her brother Paulo, her cousin Cesare? She found a certain comfort in the thought that her Rosa would take care of her sister's birthright as she herself had always been taken care of by Nina.

So, half way through life, following her path as her native bard had followed his, she left the land she loved and had come to know only too well, to start a new life in England, whose charming woodlands would prove to be her own *selva oscura*. Dark and full of shadows.

Changing her name as she changed her country was natural under the circumstances, but it was also a necessity. *Levi* was already left behind, and *Nina* was fading, there being no one around her any longer who called her by that name. However, it was on her second marriage, to Alfred William Sheldrake, that she finally became *Anna,* Anna Sheldrake, the Italian woman, the "bloody foreigner".

Looking back on her life before she came to England forever, Anna remembered often Enrico Levi, her first husband, whom she loved dearly and whom she continued to love. She loved him more in her memory and in his absence than when his physical presence was part of their everyday life. Carnal desire was not her idea of love and many philosophers would agree with her. A husband would be of a different opinion, as her husband was. She must have acquiesced to the ritual of intercourse as part of her duty as wife and out of "love" for her lawful-wedded husband. Otherwise there would have been no need for the apparatus in its box on top of the wardrobe and the small linen towel under her pillow. The hygienics of the vaginal douche went further than mere washing. She cleansed her mind as well as her body.

Cleansing a memory needs constant attention. Perhaps even more so if the memory is of a kind that needs to be forgotten. That is for the needs of life as life proceeds from day to day. At night, it must be said, another kind of memory takes over. A scene may repeat itself, not wanting to be dimmed or relegated to the realm of mere shadows, wanting to preserve its pristine colours, enhancing them even to make sure the fading process be retarded, to prevent their image eroding on the rock and so become illegible. An image can surely be read, like a book. In *The Natural History of Experience*, we might turn the pages to gaze at an etching of a fossil that appeals to us, while another page is quickly passed by choice or by chance.

I do not think Anna had nightmares. She was too strong-willed to allow such wildness. The memory of the deed perpetrated on her forced itself into her remembrance. It would emerge in a word, an opinion, a fantasy and in those very same purification rituals: in the zealous observance of these rituals you would have thought she adhered to her husband's faith. They were performed with a certain religious fervour rather than with the desperation of a sleep-walking queen.

She loved him and she knew he wished for a child, an heir, who could nevertheless never bear his Jewish heritage. He loved her so strongly, that such a love must bring forth a child. Yet she was afraid. And for them both it was a dilemma.

When did they meet? And how? I think he just saw her, at the races perhaps where she would accompany her father. There was no come-hither look from her. He had simply to pursue her until she accepted that he was serious. His mother's opposition to his besotted choice increased his fervour, and his proposal of marriage against the wishes of the Yiddish mother, against the reason of religious boundaries, convinced Signorina D'Offizi of young Signor Levi's most honourable intentions. She would show his mother what a prize her son had won; that she was a gift, to be accounted with, to be feared and in no way an object of shame.

He was 27 when they married. She was 36, with long plaits, "like a school-girl", she would add with a little laugh. She must have looked like a child-bride in a make-believe wedding. He was already a violinist in an orchestra and a qualified doctor. She was a complete innocent for all her skepticism about men, and had never worked in her life. He did indeed love her and she gradually learned to love him. He had other women, "after all he was a man" but she was not jealous: "I was his wife. I was the one he loved". She was in certain ways relieved. His infidelities, though she would not think of them as such, cleansed her as it were of the sin of reluctance and resistance, of her lack of fidelity to what went under the name of "the marriage act". In truth, for her it was "an act", and one she felt duty-bound to perform once in a while.

For nine years they lead a blissful existence. They have a fashionable flat in Rome, looking on the Tiber, next to the Synagogue. They spend their holidays in Biarritz, Anzio, Sorrento and on the Amalfi Coast, Capri, though not Sicilia because of the intervening sea and Nina feared deep water and the very thought of being on a boat made her sea-sick. How she managed to get across the water to Capri must remain s mystery.

They had money, they had friends, the jet set on the French Riviera, Juan-les-Pins, they had a charmed life. She was always surrounded by admirers, who admired her even more for being unapproachable and irreproachable. Her husband was proud of her. They were loving towards each other in spite of, maybe even because of, her lack of desire for intimacy. They were a perfect couple. That there was no child might have sown sorrow, but it did not seem like that to those around them. Rather it perpetuated the image of the couple, of their youth, their golden age and gave an illusion of eternity. As it was, so it would be forever. The political rumblings of catastrophe could be felt under their feet, they both noticed the trembling. But they would be safe. As if joy in itself were a protection.

Death came first. Then, doubt and fear.

The day of the picnic was a beautiful late-summer day as such days can be in Rome, where in the afternoon a cool breeze arises, carrying the damp air from the Tiber. The delicate loveliness of early evening resulting from the low-lying sun, the rustling of leaves and the sensuous touch of dampness on the skin, often made you want to stay longer until darkness fell and the warmth was gone.

"Come with me," he asked.

"No, *caro*, it's too hot, I'm tired."

"Wear your new dress, the pale grey crêpe de chine. You are so lovely in it. And a hat against the sun. Your charming little hat."

He touched her cheek, wanting to stroke her hair – she disliked anyone touching her hair, he knew that, but his fingers forgot, filled as they were with tactile desire. He must measure each caress, control the weight of his tenderness. He wanted to enclose and crush her against his body. For ever.

"Take a jacket," she said holding one close to her, while keeping him more away.

"It's so hot.

"For later. When the wind is cold …"

"*Va bene*. I'll take it to please you. Will you come?" He pleaded her.

"No. You go. And don't forget to put on your jacket –"

"I won't. I will do it for you."

A smile as he leaves. A kiss. Blown into space.

The wind was indeed sharp that afternoon. And he did not think to put on his jacket. He was warmed by the light Roman wine. He was enjoying the light-hearted company at the picnic. He forgot Nina for a few hours. When they all left, he forgot his jacket.

He caught a chill. Followed by pneumonia.

"If I had been there...He would have put on his jacket...I would have made sure..."

But she had not been there, and she reproached herself. As if a jacket could have kept death at bay.

If she had been there, she would have wrapped him up like a child. She would have kept him safe for a while longer until the catastrophe that already could be heard in the distance, an avalanche that rumbled closer and overtook them all. All his family. She had already lost touch with them and never knew whether his mother or his sister survived. He was fortunate, meeting death in happier circumstances. Or does it make no difference? For his wife, it made a difference in as much as she never stopped blaming herself for her wifely negligence. The fate that would have been his a few years on was not within the realm of her power to change, and therefore not her responsibility, not *her* bitter regret. She should have gone with him. She would have made him put on his jacket.

When you are in the last ditch all you can do is sing, said the Irish poet and was probably referring to his own ravaged and poverty-stricken homeland. Yet they could write poetry about their sorrows, tell mad tales to forget, and they could sing. Nina's homeland was like Ireland in some places, just as poor, just as poetic. As in Ireland, many a man dreamed of America, the land of opportunity. For an Italian, America was almost 'family', named after one of their own. For the Irish, it was just over the sea, where the potato had come from that suddenly had failed them and let them starve. They wanted food. The Italian always had food. He wanted opportunity, to make money and go back home, a success. Both peoples were dreamers, adventurers, lovers and bards.

Anna, however, did not dream of America, she dreamed of England, the dreamland she had shared with her father. There lay her haven, her land of opportunity. The very name was like a lucky charm for her, its charming landscape peopled with courteous ladies and gentlemen.

As for the inhabitants of Ireland, they were a drunken, lazy lot. She thought of them much as the English thought of the Italian immigrants who came after the War, looking for work, taking jobs from British workers – the Irish were in this case generously included in the group of honest unemployed Britons, deprived of their rightful labour by the Italian intruders. For her, the reason why the English were unemployed was because they were afraid of work, as well as downright lazy. For her, the drunken Irish were not even taken into consideration.

She herself was never out of work, though often out of pocket. Because she worked hard. That was true. She was ready to try her hand at any kind of practical employment possible to a mere woman: seamstress, furrier, housekeeper, cook, ironing shirts at the local laundry, slicing and packing ham for a large food-store, anything that had fringe benefits that could be brought home and eaten was preferable. And although she cried over our impoverished state at having to eat sausages for our Christmas dinner, I rejoiced. Sausages were not our everyday fare, since the time when Anna had seen how they were made and what they were made of. Fortunately for me, the experience had been too disgusting for her to speak of in detail, so in blissful ignorance of their unappetizing beginnings, I relished them. Sausages were not considered proper food. Being forced to dine on them a source of shame in her household. For the good-for-nothing Englishman, Alfred William, sausages and mash were a favourite dish. And as a true Cockney, his eyes also lit up at the sight of bread and dripping, dripping being the congealed mass of fat that remained after frying bacon, or a roast, and which he would spread generously on his thick slices of bread in the absence of butter. Alf could not eat butter, nor drink milk, an incapacity his wife disdained as weak and unmanly along with her disgust at his male gusto over sausages and dripping.

He would drink his cocoa without milk to accompany his working-class slices, and for some reason the aversion to milk and butter did not include cheese. When there was no dripping, a wad of Cheddar cheese would come between the chunks of bread.

"Guess wot's this!" He questioned his 'posh-speaking' daughter, fresh from her convent boarding-school.

"Soap and flannel!" he could expound with a toothless grin of glee at her educated ignorance, and as he bit into his oversize tasty morsel with his gums.

On the other hand, the sight of the small gelatinous sheep brains, which Anna spread out on the butcher block, ready to be coated in egg and rolled in flour, to end up fried golden and eaten as the delicacy they were, in Italy, would make his stomach turn. His reaction, according to his wife, came from "knowing nothing" and that was why he did not know what was good for him. His reply was usually an incoherent mumble, proving that at times he definitely knew what was best for him.

Once in a while, the limited 'while' he was present in Anna's house near the Oval, near that bastion of cricketers and the colonies and class, he would act as father. He would insist on taking his daughter out on a Sunday morning. After all, she was *his* daughter too. He was married to her mother, even though Anna was not her *real* mother either, and he knew how to get his way when he hinted at what he knew and their daughter didn't, and how he could rattle his old lady when he threatened to reveal the truth of the matter. That always made him chuckle, his mouth only half open to hide the missing upper teeth, thus giving him the gaping grimace of a gargoyle.

The daughter would get indignant and hide her nervous curiosity.

"What on earth could you tell me that would make any difference to me?" – but she noticed how the threat made a difference to her mother who would cover her fear with a retaliating threat:

"You do that and I will kill you!"

Alfred William took that as a promise. As well he should. And did not press further charges. However, he did assert his fatherly right to take out his twelve-year-old daughter on a Sunday. Not to church. Though Anna was a devout Catholic and he was brought up as a regular C. of E., as he put it. Going to church on Sundays was a matter of opportunity and possibility for both of them, rather than a necessity, in spite of there being very strong admonitions from Anna's ecclesiastic leaders to attend Sunday Mass, under threat of mortal sin if you didn't. Details of that kind did not trouble Anna's sleep or her Catholic conscience. She had her God and prayed to him when she needed to, fervently, and was absolutely sure that He understood that she did not have the time nor the energy, as hard she worked, to run off to mass all the time. Any other kind of understanding would be unthinkable with her God. To make sure He got the message, she would tell him that when she prayed, she prayed deeply and from the heart. When the feeling to pray arose. Her daughter had been taught a definition of prayer that entailed raising the mind as well as the heart to God. Anna's mind had other matters to deal with.

Alf did not even think about the matter. God was God. He had learned about His existence as a child and that at times you went to church and met people after singing together with them first and listening to the Vicar, when you had to keep still. They did not have priests in their church, and considered priests rather suspect, with their saying things in Latin, a mumbo-jumbo from before the Reformation. Alfred William was not without schooling, though, wisely again, he did not share his thoughts on religious practice with his Roman Catholic wife. She was after all more Roman than Catholic. And perhaps it might be said, looking back, more a Protestant than he was.

Their daughter however, having been educated by English nuns at boarding-school in an England where logic and philosophy were inherited along with feelings and faith, actually believed by conviction, not only by persuasion that it was not only right and proper to attend Mass on Sundays, but that not doing so was a sin.

Going to the market on a Sunday morning was, therefore, no simple affair for any single one in this trio.

Alf: "I'll take her to Petticoat Lane tomorrow."

Anna: "Mm. You will have to ask her if she wants to go with you."

Daughter: "What's Petticoat Lane?"

She is playing for time. As she had learnt early in life to do with her mother in situations involving a choice between these two protagonists. She has a vague idea as to the nature of 'Petticoat Lane'; her question is to herself as to the nature of what was going on. She senses a familiar atmosphere resembling that of the 'who do you love most, mummy or daddy' type. She did not love daddy at all, yet was curious about Petticoat Lane. And her mother did not seem dead set against it for some unaccountable reason.

Anna had come into a delicate situation. She wished for no bonding between her husband and her daughter, yet the good-for-nothing father was asserting a resemblance of fatherly desire in wanting to show the child around his part of the world. Anna did not harbour prejudices about lower or upper class in the ordinary way of such prejudices. It was more again a question of whether they behaved themselves and washed themselves in the right places. That Alf was a Cockney and did not speak *proper* was not held against him, nor was Petticoat Lane any more unsuitable than weekends in the country on the estate of landed gentry. It was again a question of being treated in a respectful manner and not catching fleas, which you got as much in the country as when you went to the pictures in Clapham. Anna, born in another era and bred in another country, dealt easily with fleas: you stripped over a tub of water when you got home and gave your clothes a good shake, the fleas then falling off could be picked up from the surface of the water and crushed between two fingernails. And as to lack of respect, or the threat of being kidnapped Anna knew that Alf would look after the girl; he would be killed if he didn't. He would also be killed if he said anything to her about *not* being her father. So she was not her usual bombastic self when the idea of this outing came up.

However, it had to be on a Sunday morning, since that was when the market was, and the child to be taken out, well-raised in her convent-schools, always went to Mass on Sunday. She said she would go to a very early mass.

Mother protested that 'the child' needed her sleep on Sunday.

Father protested that it couldn't hurt if she did not go this once.

The singularity of this discussion between the two she considered, as she must, to be her parents, dazed her a little, and coupled with her curiosity about this piece of her father's childhood she decided she wanted to go with him and would miss mass to conciliate her mother.

So there they were, father and daughter, just the two of them alone, a rare occasion since she had been a toddler, which even then Anna had contrived to keep to a minimum.

It felt strange walking alongside him like this, on their way this early Sunday morning to catch the bus to Camberwell like any ordinary father and daughter. She was perhaps 12 then and almost as tall as him after his slipped disc had changed his gait into a stoop. She kept a certain distance as they hurried to the bus-stop. The fact that he had a walking stick to support him made the gap between them less obvious as something contrived on her part. And she definitely did not want him jolting against her. When the bus came it was nearly empty so they could sit facing each other downstairs. He would not have gone upstairs anyway with his stick. Upstairs there were only double seats. He had no problem going upstairs with his walking stick at home. One day when she had let herself in after school, he was standing on the landing at the top of the first flight of stairs, threatening Anna, while Anna threatened back that she would kill him like a dog, and, she added with the full force of blind faith, the judge would not send her to prison because it would be a *crime passionnel*. Anything involving her passions were warranted under that term. Her daughter had her doubts about this interpretation of the law, as well as her apprehensions about punishment since the death penalty was still working well in England, for *crimes passionnels* in particular. After all, what else drove a human being to destroying another of the same species if not 'passion'?

They did not inform her what the quarrel had been about; the threats lead a life of their own creeping down the narrow stairway, hanging heavy in the dark hall, weighing on her mind for a very long time.

As soon as they got off the bus, Alfred William changed. He recognized the main road and quickened his step. He smiled his half-toothless smile, became buoyant in spite of his stick, which then made sharper the more frequent clicks on the pavement. There was not much traffic yet.

For his daughter, the empty streets reflected the vague emptiness inside her. Not having been to mass made this Sunday a non-Sunday. There was a blank-space in it, which was being filled with this unwonted Sunday trip to the Sunday market with her father whom she did not like to think of in that way - as a father. The very idea of the intimacy of such a relationship, with him, invoked discomfort.

For Alf, this *was* Sunday. This was what he would look forward to as a child, - he and his brother Charley, being taken by their Dad to the stalls and getting a glass of Sasspirila, if they behaved themselves. He never talked about his father except as one who put the fear of God into them all.

She thought that this is what Sundays must be like for non-Catholics. For them, the fear of God was something human. If you did a wrong deed the punishment was practical and immediate: Alf, for example, feared the belting his Dad meted out on God's behalf, with a few ungodly words thrown in as a human touch. Usually he got away with a swipe at his head, but he had seen 'the works' done on his brothers.

However, this had no real meaning for the daughter, who had never had a good hiding in her life. Her mother would sometimes bemoan the terrible time when she had slapped her child in anger, and how she would never get over that. Whereas the child could not for the life of her remember it. At times, she tried to stop the eternal recurrence of Anna's self-recriminations by suggesting that a quick slap might be preferable to the renewed mental swipes at age-old wrongdoings. Gradually she reconciled herself to mother's breast-beating. It was perhaps her personal form of the Confessional, since divine restitution to peace of mind did not fit in with her work burden.

As far as the daughter could see, it was different in general if you were a Protestant. You could do different things on a Sunday morning, because you didn't have to fit in going to Church first, under the vigilance of an avenging angel. Nevertheless, although she could grasp the inkling of freedom implicit in this possibility, there was another discomforting feeling in the cavity of her chest, that of something lost.

As I write down these memories of faded sights and smells and sounds which have necessarily disappeared after half a century, I realize that memory itself is covering another loss. Time and place transfuse into entities of uncertainty, bringing confusion, and in that confusion I must question the fragments I thought were clear-cut, actual scenes. As facts. Like an old photograph. The figures, unmoving and silent, recognizable only because their flesh and blood representations had been known for more than the flash of exposure time needed for the eye to see what the mind had already seen and passed on. The streets and buildings like relics or skeletons. The air, the wind, the penetrating damp of London rain, the stale smell of cheap smoke from Alf's overcoat, its oppressive proximity, his clicking false-teeth, put in because for him this was an occasion, the lack of synchronicity in our walking together – where were we? In the bubble of sensation I drew out of my brain (the organ in which it appeared to be stored) I recalled a wet Sunday road near Camberwell, past Kennington Park, (or was it Camberwell Green?)

on our way to his childhood's treat, to a market which proved to be as much a side-show as a place for selling one's wares.

I can see us clearly pushing our way through a small crowd that had gathered to hear a convincing quack recounting the story behind his grotesque display of large jars with what looked like broad tagliatelle floating in liquid the colour of the bitter laxative popular at my last boarding-school each Saturday morning and made from senna-pods, and which were fastened to a spot on the inside of the lid. He was, it proved, trying to sell his system and services for the removal of tapeworms. The worms captured in the jars were those he had removed from famous people, who would willingly, he claimed, recommend him in gratitude. He lavished his claims with detailed descriptions of their sufferings. Whether they were living or dead I cannot recall, and that was neither here nor there. The worms themselves were supposedly living witnesses as they danced gracefully in their fluid for their master in front of the throng of spectators. He did not seem to be selling anything other than his art.

His companion's fascination and nausea tickled Alf. He had managed to make an impression on his clever little daughter.

The two of them pushed on through the crowded Lane to single out the squash-machine that made his delectable drink. There it was with a few urchins and elderly women queuing beside it. It looked like frothy blackcurrant squash through the glazed opening high up on one of its sides.

"It looks like ordinary blackcurrant".

"Sassparila", he called it.

"Taste it," he said.

She hesitated, not keen on sweet squash for the moment, and not entirely convinced that the metal beakers hanging from chains around the impressive squash-maker could be sufficiently cleaned in their swift dip into the accompanying container of hot water. Dad swilled his portion down greedily when it was his turn and handed the cup to her. The colour was more like redcurrant in the beaker and there was a lot of pale froth on top. The taste was unexpected, not sweet but slightly tangy and refreshing, and she forgot about possible contamination. Sixpence-a-go.

In my present-day efforts to piece the puzzle of these fragments onto some shape of a true picture, I searched for information as to whether it really had existed, this East-end elixir that had excited my father's own reminiscence of a taste and a treat. Finally, I discovered *sarsparilla*, which had not degenerated into 'sassparila' from ignorant pronunciation, but was in fact pronounced that way and originated from a Mexican herb, indispensable as a blood-purifier among its qualities, also a palliative to the sufferings of syphilis. Had he mentioned it was good for the blood? It is possible. And equally possible that I being in no way interested at that age in such remedies took the information as trying to impress or trying to be funny. 'Sarsparilla' did exist and I had wormed it out of my memory of that day. But which market did we visit? Was there a market in Camberwell of the kind I clearly see in my mind? Maybe it was not Camberwell at all, though Camberwell sticks in my mind when I think of him and that day, and deflects into refusal at the thought that he might have taken me to several different places, and which I have moulded into one for convenience. I must admit that for years I believed Petticoat Lane to be situated in Camberwell. Is that where I lost track? Along Kennington Lane? Only five minutes from home yet in unfamiliar country?

Petticoat Lane started life as Middlesex Street, or Hogs Lane, the latter name probably because pigs were allowed to be kept there, or were driven in that direction, outside the city back in Tudor times. Then cottages were built and the Spanish ambassador to James I had his house there with resulting popularity for other Spaniards until the Great Plague drove them away or killed them off. By then the area had begun to trade in second-hand clothes and bric-a-brac and thus became 'Petticote Lane', not a suitable word for the Victorians, concerned as they were with double-lives, upstairs and downstairs, overcoats and underwear, and it was changed back to Middlesex Street, a suitable compromise.

Alfred William talked often about Petticoat Lane Market, extolling its virtues such as they surely had appeared to an impoverished Cockney lad looking for free entertainment and cheap refreshments. After the Great War he was just going on 20 and the crowds and illicit atmosphere would have attracted him, not to joining in with anything illegal, but not adverse to napping bits and pieces if the police were diverted to deal with real trouble. He was too timid to be a troublemaker on his own initiative, and his mother, too, had put a certain fear of God into him in her way.

'The Lane' is situated in the vicinity of Liverpool Street Station, where Alfred William worked, first as a porter then as an attendant in the Left Luggage Office. All the years he had used transporting the trunks and cases of the well-to-do on his trolley took their toll on his back and when a slipped-disc and lumbago made it impossible for him to exert himself in that manner, they gave him a job looking after forgotten items. Once he had taken his daughter with him to the Christmas Staff Party. She had not wanted to go, of course, but in this her mother, surprisingly, encouraged his wishes. So, unwillingly, again driven by a certain curiosity and suspense, she had accompanied him.

When they arrived they were instantly surrounded by his work-mates, female as well as male, who were clearly on friendly terms with 'Alf' or 'Sheldrake' and gave him all the credit for his 'luvly' daughter. The 'luvly' daughter was in a quandary as how to behave. Apart from the usual teenage discomfort of being ogled and examined as to dress, looks and age, came the unexpected situation in which she could see that Alf was, if not the life and soul of the party, very much at home with his Railway station mates in a way that made him appear, strange to say – jolly. Under these circumstances, she could not treat him as she was used to doing at home, that would be exposing herself, but she had to keep up a certain aloofness so he wouldn't get any wrong ideas. However, a convent-school upbringing, coupled with shyness and gaucherie in a pretty dress saved her from revealing her intense discomfort. They were a talkative bunch, so her polished speech did not shame her in this school of East-enders. A surprised office boss or two was dragged over to be introduced, and lingered.

Yes. He *had* taken her to Petticoat Lane, renowned for the way its vendors would demonstrate their skills. Crockery, to take one example, would be piled high, thrown into the air and caught on the way down. Almost without a breakage. And renowned for the patter which accompanied their demonstrations, like the tape-worm show. But in some devious way the bus they had taken had passed through the Camberwell I remembered from that Sunday, cloudy with a bit of rain.

In my efforts to straighten out these unsettling knots of forgetfulness, I came across Walnut Tree Grove, in Camberwell. Our little old lady next door who attended *Walnut Tree Walk School* so diligently, must have once lived nearby and had not moved far in her transition to married life. Nor had Alfred William moved far. Anna had had him in tow around the English countryside for a few years until she sent him away. When she moved back to London, she ran him to earth, though a willing prey, routed him out again and brought him back to home ground from where ever he had been in those intervening years. He did not talk about it. You could believe he had not been away. He did not speak about the War either, except to mention a building that had been there before the bombing. Nor did he speak of his time in Burma, where during the Second World War he had been a prisoner. Perhaps the very distance made it unreal.

But of that I knew nothing at the time, only that he was a pathetic figure, suffering the darts and arrows aimed at him by his outrageous wife and daughter. He suffered them in silence, or at most with an expressive grunt. He sat in his pyjamas in the middle of the day at his corner of the living room table, rolling cigarettes with his cigarette-roller, his hands shaking and his fingers yellowed. His daughter disliked his 'state of undress', especially the night-time smell of it, but liked making cigarettes for him with the little machine, and would make a pile until she got it right. He was pleased and patient. He was to be pitied. They both were.

Was she twelve, or thirteen? Or less? This daughter he took to the Market and to the Staff Dance? Was it before he left them, or was it after he had come back? 'Left' and 'come back' are not *les mots justes*: 'sent away – again' and 'brought back'- again, are more the case. He was brought back into grace, you might say, because Anna needed him, and also because she did in fact genuinely pity him.

"Just a poor fellow. After all, what can I do?" She would say with her usual rhetoric, mixing forgiveness, soft-heartedness and severity, with an underlying appeal for her actions to be understood.

Times passed, and places displaced twirl round in my brain at a dizzying speed the more I try to stop shaking the kaleidoscope full of these tiny coloured cuttings, like torn butterfly wings that smoulder between your fingers. What went on, what actually happened, become moving images in the way a statue under the sea, or a shipwreck, or a sunken city will fluctuate when we gaze down at them through the waves.

So, how did it come to this?

That the beautiful, desirable Nina D'Offizi, Signora Enrico Levi, covered by her adoring husband in pearls and diamonds, should become Anna Sheldrake, with a good-for-nothing Englishman, a Cockney, absent from her side as she worked her fingers to the bone to give her daughter a good education, while constantly wracked with worry as to whether her health hold long enough so she would be able to work, to earn sufficient money to keep a roof over their heads and food on the table, hold long enough for her daughter to grow old enough to take over, earning good money with all her education, and then could take care of *her*.

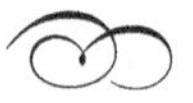

5

Along with Anna's other country came another family.

The family Sheldrake were an old family as much as the D'Offizis were, but then genetically all families are old, and if their wanderings could be traced, many unexpected relationships might be established. The Sheldrakes were around at the same time as Richard the Lionhearted, one of them registered in the 'Pipe rolls of Essex' as a Lord of the Manor. They had a family crest then: three ducks on a shield and a fourth duck on the top of the armour helmet. John Sheldrake was born in 1564, the same year as William Shakespeare, and in 1732 Elizabeth Sheldrake left for the New World as a bonded passenger, which probably meant that work was not to be found for her in the South East of England.

From landed gentry in Essex to working class in Middlesex and from there to the East End of London took a few hundred years, until all class transitions were speeded up in the eighteenth century. Many climbed rapidly up ladders of pecuniary progress, and many, as they endeavoured to keep standing at the top, fell, hard. From a distance, history's time-span, Anna and Alf were not as different as they themselves thought they were. They had both fallen from heights, and it no longer mattered whether their respective coats-of-arms had helmets topped with a crown or with a merry duck.

'Sheldrake' was the result of a nickname, not a place, and suggests its owner was a vain fellow. There is a record in 1275 in Suffolk of an Adam le Sceldrake who must have looked on himself as a leading man. Centuries later, Alfred William rapidly turned into a dandy with Anna's taste and money.

"He never had a clean shirt before he met me. Now he has twenty. And he thinks he is a millionaire."

His treatment of his socks brought down more disdain:

"Before, he had nothing. Now when there's a hole in one sock he throws away the pair. He cannot appreciate nothing – nothing that I do for him!"

Here, she relapsed into a double negative with apt poetic license, as it doubled the incomprehensible negativity involved in his action.

"Because it's *my* money. He doesn't have to earn it..."

He had already given away Anna's long string of perfect pearls to a woman he had met at the local pub, who knew how to appreciate his generous rounds of drinks, and who was unaware that those pearls represented the remaining fortune of Alf's 'rich' wife, who had repeatedly given them all reason for a good laugh. Anna, too, was to be pitied. Pity, however, was not what she was interested in.

Then there was Alf's family.

"When I met him they were so charming. Doing everything for me. Oh Anna, here and oh Anna there. Then, when I married him, suddenly they were gone. I never saw them again. I understood very soon they were glad to be rid of him. He was a liability for them. Ah well, what could I do then? A woman alone?"

Indeed, what *could* she do? Those who really loved her were far away and in addition lived in a country soon at war with England. She had secured an English surname for herself and had not as yet qualified for the title of "bloody foreigner". Alfred William had thus fulfilled his primary role: making her a British citizen and as such she could not be deported. Her inborn distrust of authorities made her sceptical as to whether the ship delegated to carry Italian nationals out of Britain when the war finally broke out would ever make it across the Atlantic Sea.

She remembered well what had happened before. On 1 May 1915, the *Lusitania* sailed from New York to Liverpool with 2000 passengers on board and, when rounding the Irish coast, it was torpedoed by German U-boats. The German Embassy in Washington had issued a public warning to potential passengers to the effect that Germany was at war with Britain and that her coastal waters were also war territory. Despite a considerable unease amongst both passengers and crew, the warning was not heeded and on 7th May 1915 the luxury liner was attacked and went down in the course of eighteen minutes.

In 1915, on the last day of May, Anna turned twenty-six.

Three years previously, in 1912, on 10th April the *Titanic* had left Southampton for New York. Four days later she went down after hitting an iceberg on an unusually calm sea under the moonless night sky. During those last hours and minutes before the disaster was consummated many messages went unheeded. The telegraphists were too busy as intermediaries for prominent guests who were delighting in making use of technological progress to call all and sundry, too busy with the carefree enjoyment of life on a luxury liner to pay enough attention to the desperate warnings from crew to the captain and to let them through. They went unheeded.

In 1912, Anna was still an innocent, whose doting uncle, the monsignor with the family's seat in the Vatican, had chosen to accompany him to New York, where he was to give a sermon in St. Patrick's Cathedral. His niece would be company for him and the trip would be an experience for her. Anna was not only an innocent: she was a thinking innocent. And she was not jumping with joy at the prospect of a long sea voyage. She had a great respect for her uncle and was acutely aware of the honour he was bestowing on her. She was, however, terrified of the sea and suffered horribly from seasickness. Her uncle's assurances about the safety of such a large and modern ship and that it was built so that she could not possibly get sick did nothing to convince her. This was a maiden voyage. Before she would set her foot on board she would see how the first crossing went. Monsignor had a sermon to deliver so for him there was no question about it. They had to board that ship, on that day.

Anna's motto, her mantra you might call it, "Actions speak louder than words", had become her guide early in life. She had no argument strong enough to counter the sermon in the Cathedral. Instead, she locked herself in her hotel room. There she stayed while her uncle pleaded, ranted and raved outside her door. Nothing would make her open that door until the ship had left and was well on its way. She did not fear his anger nor his less-than-doting behaviour. She had got her way. The *Titanic* had sailed away and she was no longer worried.

On Monday, 15th April the news broke. Anna was proved right. A very subdued cleric found her at breakfast and thanked her.

"He cried and he thanked me," she would say when she told her tale later in life. She did not gloat. She understood his anger and helplessness at not being able to leave her alone in Southampton and embark alone. However, he must after the event realize that her disobedience had been for his own good.

When the *Arandora Star* sank off the coast of Ireland on 2nd July 1940, the news of this calamity did not come as a surprise to Anna. She had predicted the danger with her Cassandra's curse and deep fear of the sea.

The *Arandora Star* was a luxury liner from the Blue Star Line. The *Titanic* was a White Star cruise ship. The innovations and luxurious interiors of the *Titanic* had sought to compete with the opulence of the *Lusitania*, which had been built by the Cunard Line. Both were for transatlantic crossings, as was the *Arandora Star.* The White Star Line did not christen their ships, contrary to usual practice. In the uproar of disbelief and suffering that followed the impossible sinking of the *Titanic*, certain voices were raised to suggest that the lack of a proper christening had sent her to her doom.

As regards the *Arandora Star*, no one suggested that that disaster was written in those stars, White or Blue. It was clearly man-made. German-made. And any anger that might have been turned to the gods was turned towards them. It was a turning point in public opinion. On Tuesday 2nd July 1940, Britain became anti-German.

Since the rise of Mussolini and his closer relationship with Hitler, Italians in Britain were becoming gradually more foreign, until 11th June 1940 when Italy came into the war on the wrong side. The British War Cabinet decided "to round up undesirable aliens who could pose a threat to Britain, disregardless of how long, how well integrated". Winston Churchill's words were: "Collar the lot!" The undesirable aliens were Austrian and Italian as well as German. People who had been living in England or Scotland for over forty years like the popular Italian ice-cream manufacturers and shop owners in especially the Northern counties were sent to Liverpool to board ship on 1st July, not knowing when they might return.

Already the next day, their friends, and the families they had married into, knew. Of the 1,500 internees and POWs on board, 670 would never return. 470 of these were Italian men.

Arandora Star, this beautiful ocean liner that had cruised the Mediterranean in the '30's before Anna had left Italy, and who had spent the winter of 1938 in the waters round Panama. Cuba, Mexico and the West Indies, who had visited the Norwegian Fjords, where Anna ended up in her old age, the age her father had promised would never come to her, this once-wealthy world traveller, as she was about to leave the North Sea, as she rounded the coast of County Donegal, was torpedoed by German submarines.

She had started her career as plain *Arandora*, after being launched on 1st April 1927. She had sailed for a few years around the coast of South America when she was brought into dock once more and refitted as should become a *Star.* She was a real beauty in white paint with a scarlet band around her hull, like a silk ribbon, which gave her the nicknames 'Wedding Cake' or 'Chocolate Box'. During those sunny and star-lit years, she would sail from Southampton, as befitted so majestic a sight. When war broke out she did duty as a transport ship, evacuating troops from France and Norway, returning disguised in dull grey.

The *Star* left from Liverpool, bound for Canada, in her camouflage colour, unescorted, and as it proved lacking a Red Cross sign that showed that there were prisoners and civilians on board. Her grey attire was given as one reason why she was mistaken for a military vehicle. There were less innocent reasons. The German submarine captain had fallen into the shadow of one of his junior officers, who had been awarded for the high number of hits he had carried out against enemy ships. The *Arandora Sta*r was a godsend to this captain. She sailed right across his home-bound trajectory. He took her like a *demi mondaine*, the victim of the spoils of war. Prestige and envy have always caused trouble.

She had once been the most famous ship in the world, and on 2nd July, in the second year of the Second World War, in the course of her dowdy-dressed duty, she was shot and reeling over with her bows stuck up into the air she went to the bottom of the sea in the course of thirty-five minutes.

The coast of Ireland is littered with memorials to those who died in that terrible hour.

Anna tried to be fair in her judgements. After her fashion. The *Titanic* had been on her maiden voyage and therefore any claims to being "unsinkable" had first to be proved. In fact, it was the press that introduced that notion – after the event. Always an advocate for Italian engineering, and intelligence in general, Anna would often remind her listeners that it was Marconi who invented the telegraph, a fact people often forgot, in her opinion. What would she have said if she had known that the telegraphists on the *Titanic* had been employed by Marconi for the service of the passengers and thus had ignored crew messages to the bridge on the impending danger. Even so, Marconi was thanked for his invention. Its signals had in the end contributed to many being saved.

The *Lusitania* had been sailing under a white flag, yet was attacked. Although the Germans had issued warnings to potential passengers, they were to blame. "Cold-blooded", was Anna's judgment. The *Arandora Star* had carried no white flag. Who was to blame for that? Anna blamed the British. Did she know that there were British soldiers on board to guard the POWs and that these soldiers were ordered to shoot at the life-boats to prevent their prisoners from escaping? Even if the flag was a mistake, she had reason to blame the British. They even blamed themselves. The Committee of Inquiry which published its findings before Christmas the same year criticized the War Cabinet for deporting indiscriminately Fascist and non-Fascist Italians alike.

Maybe Anna was one of those rare individuals who learn from history and from those lessons make up their own minds. She had left Italy because of what she saw was happening there. She could guess which direction those events were going. She had no intention of being sent back. She had been married to a Jew. And however intelligent Mussolini might have been considered, she did not trust him. Or anyone else for that matter.

The Sheldrake family were not to be trusted either. But they did not represent any danger to her. "They are simple." She only observed that they were glad to be rid of the simplest among them. It made her angry, but in a way she could understand them. When all came to all, *she* was the one who had hoodwinked them. She had needed their name to protect her. Probably she forgot that when she realized that her simple husband was not happy to be just a name.

He had had a short bout of happiness, albeit bliss, at his luck in landing a catch like Anna. Well-off and good-looking. He was unaware of the shadow side of the enthusiasm his relatives showed at his beginner's luck. That Anna might have any motive other than the natural desire for husband and family, never entered his mind. Her cool responses to his physical approaches did not daunt him. At first.

"I'll make you love me," he would say, confident in his powers of seduction.

"Yes, yes," she might reply, or "Mmm" or some similar sound of non-committal agreement. How could he have even imagined it. How could he in month of Sundays come upon the idea that she had chosen him from among several keen candidates for the very reason that she knew she never *could* love this man. Alfred William was simple in his nature as much as in his mental capacities. One side was pleasing, the other side nasty. Her argument was that if she should come to feel love for a man, or respect him enough to be forced to take his feelings into account, she would be betraying Enrico, who had truly loved her, "adored" was her word. She would have to force herself to overcome her repulsion for physical contact with a male. "Sexual" was not a word she would voice, or consciously think.

In spite of all these cross motives, cross purposes, expectations and disappointments, explicit or unknown, family was family and as far as it was possible, Anna followed her line of duty. One of these duties was a visit to Alf's brother George. Was it George? Did Alf have a brother by that name? He had two brothers and, vaguely, a sister. Brother Charley had emigrated to Canada, so he was not the one, and strange to think that *his* name cropped up often, perhaps because he was the one Alf felt closer to when they were kids together, or perhaps just because he was so far away that the childhood camaraderie remained untouched. There were no letters from Canada. The sister, Winnie, was only a name. Had she sickened and died young? Had she been much older or much younger so that Alf's life and hers were only linked by the parents? Yet he did linger over her name with a kind of softness. As he would when he talked of his mother, which was not often and to tell the same story, of her putting-him-to-bed ritual: she would sit by his bed until he fell asleep, with his hands crossed over his heart and, most important, above the covers, the implications of which were then, and seemed to be still whenever he spoke of it, unclear. The image evoked resembled the image of death reproduced on the sarcophaguses of the rich or the famous in old churches. And Alfred William gave no sign of their being any unspoken-of reason to go to sleep in this way other than that it was the admonition and bed-time prayer of a caring mother, an accepted ritual to protect him through the dangers of the night.

George or not George, a visit was made to Alf's brother by Anna and her daughter, unaccompanied by Alfred William. It must have been before the excursion to Petticoat Lane, before his forced return.

Anna announced the visit, as a seemingly conventional observance, although her observances were always of her own invention, that of a sister-in-law performing her duty, however distasteful that duty might be. And it was distasteful enough.

The actual name of the district in which George resided is forgotten. That it was a dark and dirty place is memorable. George himself, George with a question mark, George who else could he be when that is the name that remains of Alf's brother who was not Charley, - George himself emerged memorably from this dark and dirty place, first as a slight movement of the colours of dark and the shadows of a once light-coloured shirt with no collar. He moved out of the shadows of his grey kitchen. Shrunken, toothless, more than Alf, unshaven, harmless, helpless.

He shuffled about and brought out two cups, which he placed on the table next to his own mug. While he went to put the kettle on for the traditional "cupper", Anna gave the cups an extra wash, discreetly, drying them with the man-size handkerchief which she always kept in her handbag. She gave up trying to remove the brown stains embedded in the chips and cracks. In such matters, accepting another's hospitality, weighed against her wish to be able to drink the tea offered, Anna did not overdo it. She was kind-hearted, and had no intention of offending the old man in his blatantly miserable state: all she wanted was to avoid that she and her daughter should fall ill from some hidden contamination. Stepping down the one-step into George's very small kitchen and living room felt like a step into another age, of impoverishment, of Dickensian misery brought about by fate and foolishness.

In what way George had been foolish, will remain unknown.

In my memory, the contours of the room into which we had entered by way of an entrance now forgotten, from a forgotten street in some faded area of the one of Dickens' two cities, fade into darkness, a fuzzy periphery framing the focus of our visit, this old man at his kitchen table, his once-hardworking fingers curled round his thick mug of dark sweet tea, as if he too were clinging to a memory. In my mind, the image of George mingles with that of Balzac's old Goriot, in the other city on the other side of the Channel, sitting at *his* table covered with its greasy oil-cloth, where the original colours were no longer visible, waiting, waiting for his beloved daughter. Did George have a daughter? And did she care as little for him as Goriot's daughter cared for him? Was that why we were visiting? Anna, ever sensitive of a parent's longing for the absent child, would nevertheless have disputed Balzac's claim that the father's love for a daughter was the most pure form of love.

George's room was dimensioned similar to the one in which we ourselves lived at that time, near the Oval Underground Station; the living-room of the place of our own of which Anna had dreamed and worked hard for, for many years. Our English house and garden was in the nitty-gritty of it constructed with the bricks and mortar of Britain's industrial expansion, which had expressed itself in row after row of Englishmen's castles, squeezing their proud gardens out behind them around stone back-yards like pig-tails, twisted words, ironic metaphors, the opium of the hard-working classes.

The materialization of her home-dream was no disappointment to Anna, the mistress of survival of the fittest, and keeper of the seal of future attainment. She had no reason to feel disappointed. She had plans. Her daughter, with none of her mother's experience of life and its meandering ways, saw her picture of a manor in miniature surrounded by a lawn and flowers, rather like *The Secret Garden* only smaller, smudged over with charcoal, and torn up as a failure. Its proportions were those of George's den, not those of the long-awaited sovereign abode and a room-of-her-own.

6

Roll out the barrel, We'll have a barrel of fun... or as the original Czech version called it, *The Beer-Barrel Polka*, a soldier song that had travelled through Germany and became a hit in England in June 1939. That was when Nina married Alfred William Sheldrake and became, once and for ever, Anna.

The marriage took place at the Registrar's Office in Kensington and they may have gone to the local pub to celebrate. Piano-playing and sing-a-longs were as part and parcel of pub-life as were darts. There would certainly have been a chorus of *Roll out the barrel* and Anna would have joined in as she enjoyed her glass of beer. Or Guiness, which she preferred. It would not have marred the taste if she had known it was from an Irish brewery. Nor did she need the encouragement of advertising posters to tell her that 'Guiness is good for you', with the portrait of a huge glass of the black liquid topped with creamy brown froth, in which a smiling face looked at you like the man-in-the-moon. She used it for both nutritional and medicinal purposes. Believing, and rightly so, that babies should sleep at night, she would feed her baby daughter a spoonful of Guiness with sugar as a somniferous potion. Soup-spoon or tea-spoon dosage, she could boast that *her* child never woke up and cried in the night.

Anna loved singing. She would sing around the house, often those catchy wartime tunes. They were part of her transposition from Italy to England. From champagne to beer.

She had trained as a singer. A training, which must have taken place after her dancing years in the corps de ballet. She travelled with the troupe to Buenos Aires and to Moscow. Buenos Aires was a beautiful city. And Moscow. Her vivid memory from Moscow was a very early morning when she had met a baker with a tray of his goods held high. Warm damp rose up and his apron was covered in flour. She had stopped to look at him and he had given her a bun. Oh, it tasted so good. She had crept out of the hotel before anyone was awake, to have a look around for herself. That must have been in 1902 before the first Russian rising, when Nina was about 12 years old and when her father was still alive. Naturally he had a Nanny to look after his children, whatever Nina might believe about her own position at her father's side as some sort of consort rather than a daughter. Naturally, Nanny must accompany his daughter on tour in the wide world, and young Rosa must have been cared for by a substitute. To Nina, Nanny was 'hers'.

When her time in the children's *corps de ballet* came to an end, she turned to singing. To opera. She was a contralto. The distinction between 'contralto' and 'soprano' was mostly lost on those to whom she imparted this information.

At the time, the 1950's, during the first period of her 'own-home-at-last' project between the Kennington-Oval and Brixton, there were not, in her vicinity, many opera-lovers. So, when a musician-couple rang the doorbell, asking to see the bed-sitter that was to let on the first floor, she was persuaded, without excessive compunction, to take them in. "We're not married" had brought a frown to her eyes.

"Ah, but what can I do?", she would say, both to those who knowing her expressed surprise, and to herself, repeating this password of appealing rhetoric which popped up whenever she acted against her beliefs and which was intended to keep away the Furies, like a self-service confessional exonerating her from her sin.

The sinful couple must also exonerate themselves. The woman, an Australian, had come to England for further tuition to improve her singing technique. The man was English and a pianist and her accompanist. He had been the more enthusiastic of the two in wanting to rent the room, knowing more than his companion what an English bed-sitter usually looked like. This room was the best in the house: large, full of light, or more correctly, full of the light available in the smoggy London of the time, because it was on the first floor facing the street, and it had a piano. Little did he know that the greatest advantage may suddenly turn and become the greatest disadvantage. And being allowed to rent this room-cum-piano had a condition attached.

The condition was that he had to give free piano lessons to the landlady's twelve- year-old daughter, who had been without a "proper teacher" since being wrenched out of her last boarding school, where they had prepared their piano pupils for examinations at The Royal Academy of Music. The prospective lodger's protests that he was not trained as a music teacher and had absolutely no experience with teaching children were to no avail. Just as the protests of the local church organist had been overruled: that the organ and the piano were two different instruments. The latter lessons, which had to take place in church on an organ that some innocent church-worker had to pump while lessons were carried out, soon dwindled out, a relief to all except to Anna. In her educational plan, her daughter must learn all the skills she might come to need later in life, and one of them was piano playing. She might once have had an image of a soirée in a genteel drawing-room, but that had been long replaced by an understanding that the world had changed.

"If you need money you will always be able to get a job playing in a public bar", was her resounding reason for the ever-present piano in their not well-to-do home.

"I don't want you to have to work hard 16 hours a day like me."

The boarding-school educated child hoped there might be a few other alternatives between "doctor or lawyer," the necessary results of the good education, and "pub-pianist".

The organist had understood that both he and his pupil were joined in forced labour and, accordingly, kind man that he was, did what he had to do with great patience. The shanghaied lodger was not a patient man. And since Anna blamed him as the male and thus dominated by own desires, for the illicit relationship between him and his quiet lady friend, he appropriately was to suffer most. And consequently, his student suffered with him.

He was indeed no teacher, and although he had emphatically conveyed this fact to his landlady, she did not believe him. She had heard him play. He played well, full of fire and delicacy. He was English. False modesty was *comme il faut.*

His pupil came like a lamb to the slaughter. With her, he was only fire, interspersed with flashes of utter boredom, which were no relief to the lamb, who knew these silences preceded a kill. With each wrong note she played, and there were increasingly many, she sensed that a cauldron inside him was beginning to bubble and boil until it boiled over into sounds in a language definitely not fit for children, nonetheless with an undertone understandable at any age. Her fumbling tempo turned his face red and his features became a mask of both fire and brimstone. He would take a rapid turn around the sofa like a classical Japanese actor, muttering to himself.

When he could no longer bear the acoustic pain of these penal meetings he saw no alternative but to give his notice. By the time they left, a month later, the pupil's ignorant enjoyment of her own impromptu albeit enervating piano-playing was all but wiped out. The frugal ability remaining from convent days had to be restored under her own auspices and those of the long-suffering and doting mother, and she indulged in long-drawn out versions of melancholy Scottish songs.

What were their names, these protagonists in this short musical interlude? Bill and Jane? Or was it Sarah? Jane-Sarah was a shadow of big Bill. Her name, whichever it was, laced his conversations with his landlady ensuring her ever-presence, while most of her waking hours she spent at lessons with some maestro or other 'downtown'. 'Downtown' made central London sound foreign, and was perhaps for her a bit of nostalgia reminding her of back home in Australia.

Jane-Sarah was a contralto, like Anna. Her idol, her reason for travelling across the world to damp and cloudy Britain, in part perhaps drawn and pushed by Bill, her inspiration and driving force was Kathleen Ferrier. There was a biography of Ferrier propped up on the mantelpiece with a few other books behind it. On the cover was a pensive portrait of the singer. The first book written about her came out in 1954, after she had died from cancer only half a year before, in October 1953. The cover photograph was memorable and haunting. It induced the subdued pupil to dare to ask her teacher who it was. Bill, surprisingly, answered at great length. And stopped abruptly. She had been still alive when the decision to go to England had been taken. The book must have been the one by the music critic and cricketer Neville Cardus, who had for several years, lived in Australia, where cricket had truly taken root. He was born in Lancashire, cricket's home ground and came to represent a different way in writing about the game. He became a music critic by inclination and chance. Kathleen Ferrier, the 'Lass from Lancashire', well-known for her sense of humour and ribald jokes, must have been tickled pink by the contrast in Cardus' activities.

Bill introduced his pupil to the variety of teaching methods, and to perhaps not the best way to promote an enjoyment of music.

But then there was Anna. She believed in 'learning by doing', though not in the sense John Dewey had meant. In her version, she, being the embodiment of knowledge and experience, was the one to do the 'doing', while the student would learn by watching. The method is not without its acolytes and there is much to be said in its favour as to acquiring an appreciation of song, if insufficient for actually learning to sing, although she generously explained a few breathing techniques on the way. The delight of playing in a bath-tub with bubbles and plastic yellow duck to the tune of "*Bella figlia del amore...*" lasts forever.

Anna's career as an opera singer had come to a sudden end, she said, when on stage after a performance she had stood to receive the enthusiastic applause of the audience. Of all the bouquets of flowers thrown at her feet she had bent down and picked up one with beautiful roses, and buried her face in them, breathing in all their fragrance. She had lost her voice, she said. They had been sent by a jealous rival and she claimed to know the culprit.

However, although her career was over, her singing days were not. She would sing snatches of well-known and obscure opera arias, Neapolitan folksongs and catchy British hits. "*You made me love you, I didn't want to do it, I didn't want to do it..*" was another bath-time favourite. She could also burst into song in public, that is walking along the street, hand in hand with her daughter, assured that the smiles she met were from her infectious good mood, which was not always the case in for instance, Brixton Market on a Saturday morning.

Nor did she limit herself to her own parts in the operas in which she had performed. She knew, truly by heart, arias by the tenor or soprano. The great tenor performers she remembered in her own contralto version were Caruso, Benjamino Gigli, all "good men." Transposing soprano parts was more challenging and often her voice would break.

"Ah, I cannot do it anymore! But when I was young.... You should have heard me then! And Patti, and Tetrazzini, and Melba!"

These names were sounds from another world and had no other meaning for her daughter than that. Except for 'Melba', which was the name of a delicious dish experienced on one of her mother's educational restaurant expeditions, embarked on when funds permitted. It proved that the golden preserved peaches with vanilla ice-cream and raspberry sauce was first concocted for the great soprano Nellie Melba, an Australian behind the Italian name, and later a Dame. In 1892, when Anna was just a toddler, the French chef at The Savoy in London created this pudding for the celebration the Duc d'Orleans gave the singer after her success in *Lohengrin*. The original consisted of an ice swan filled with ice-cream and peaches topped with spun sugar. Outwardly a far cry from Anna's bucket of fruit kept cool in water under her pergola. However, she probably preferred the peaches in the bucket, fresh from the tree, the bloom glistening with the prisms of droplets. What concatenation of circumstances had brought Sarah-or-Jane from sunny Australia to Anna's room-to-let in a dark and dingy part of London town?

Many parts of London were dingy and always had been, although the dinginess could move around over the years. The English, Londoners especially, had this trait of character akin to Italians of finding fun in the midst of misery, an ability to poke fun at themselves. In England, one example of this was the 'music hall'. 'Little Tich' was a music hall performer Anna remembered and whose very memory made her laugh when she spoke of him. As his name suggests, he was not tall and his most famous number from 1900 was his Big Boot Dance which surely was the inspiration for Charlie Chaplin's Little Man. He was an international star already at the age of 12, and Anna may have seen him in Italy or in Paris during the 1920's or even his last appearance in London in 1927. Stravinsky claimed to be inspired by him, though in what way is unclear. He also played the Dame in that other English stage invention, the Pantomime. Not the type perfected in France, but the family event at Christmastide, where fairy-tales were acted out with Princes played by ladies with attractive legs and high-heels and the various versions of an Ugly Sister was played by a man in drag. One popular panto was *Humpty Dumpty* which in 1891 we would today say 'starred' Marie Lloyd – usually portrayed with a cherry caught on her teeth -, Dan Leno, and Little Tich. One of Marie Lloyd's songs which Anna would sing was *A little of what you fancy does you good.* For her, this applied to food, and wine, and was clearly disconnected from Marie Lloyd's insinuating smile as she was about to take the cherry into her mouth. Another song from that time, kept alive by Anna, was another artiste's invitation to the pub: *Down at the Old Bull and Bush.* At 60, still greatly popular, Little Tich went on tour to Australia. His Big Boot Dance was booed by hooligans among the audiences. He returned to England a broken man. And died within a year.

Anna was booed in another manner by her London neighbours. They did not manage to break her; they made her tougher.

She had bought a house at the Kennington-Oval - cheap, as behoved her hard-earned and limited savings. She had sufficient capital to secure the down payment and the mortgage. She felt she was getting on in years and wanted to realize her dream of a place of her own making it possible for her to live with her daughter all the time instead of slaving night and day while her child was away at boarding school.

The idea of a house for the child, who had so far lived in the English country-side, was like in a drawing, a square with a chimney, two front windows on each floor and a front-door, all surrounded by a garden with trees, a fence and a gate. The new architectural designs inspired by the needs of the workers, who inundated large towns after the Industrial Revolution, were unknown to her. The house Anna bought was three stories high and joined to at least forty others in a winding street, facing a similar line on the opposite side. The doors had different colours, and in some cases, for the more well-off, so did the paintwork round the windows. It was thus much larger than that needed for the two of them. Anna planned to have lodgers and no longer have to work 16 hours a day. There was, however, a catch. The reason why the house was relatively cheap was that those who were living on the first and second floors had no wish to move out nor to pay the rent Anna proposed. During the war rents had been regulated officially at a very low rate. The elderly lady, who was roughly the same age as Anna, living on the first floor, was protected by law, as well as by all the neighbours she had had for 30 years. Anna was undaunted.

"This is my property. I will make her life hell. She will want to leave", she proclaimed not only to her daughter, but also to the lady in question.

Whatever the methods Anna used they finally worked. The man on the top floor must have understood quickly that he was no match for this foreigner and soon disappeared. This meant that the first floor must be traversed to reach the second. After the regulated tenant left, the daughter got a room of her own for the first time, a tiny box-room with a large window looking out on all the back gardens and taking in the sun when it was showing.

It soon became the child's paradise, and the hell-fire that went to obtain it cooled. The front room which then was vacant became the bed-sitter that Bill and his Australian singer moved into. They too had had their dreams which must have been brighter than the strings attached to those lodgings. The whole house was one of dreams and dashed hopes. Yet new dreams constantly arise.

Many years previously, on yet another train journey to a new place of work where the employer offered higher wages than the previous one, and thus contributing to a more speedy accumulation of the earnings that were to make real the woman-of-property dream, Anna met another dreamer.

"Excuse me for bothering you", Anna said in her most appealing manner, honed to cause the most aloof Englishman to wish to be bothered, "Are you going to Pwllheli?" She pronounced it 'Fuelly' as they had done at the ticket office in Gloucester.

"I beg your pardon, madam?"

Anna repeated her question, equally beguiling in her manner.

"I'm afraid you must have taken the wrong train..."

"No, that is not possible," though a slight doubt had crept in.

"At the station they showed it to me on the map, and there was a picture on the wall, it was one of the most beautiful spots in Wales.."

"Well, I know Wales very well. Whereabouts is it supposed to be?"

"Right up in the North, near the sea, and the mountains..."

"Ah," He sighed clearly with relief that after all he did not have to be the harbinger of bad news to this charming foreign lady and her shy child. "Ah, you mean Pwllheli!"

"Yes," she repeated a few times emphatically, after having written the word down on his newspaper. It took her a moment to hear that he pronounced it quite differently. 'Pullkelly'. An interesting exchange of sounds followed involving an amount of saliva and mouth-twisting and laughter. Whether the child was invited to join in is not clear. It was after all an advanced language lesson, which quickly developed into an exchange of life experiences and ideas. Some linguists claim that language came first and thus accelerated the intellectual development of homo sapiens and not the other way around, and this incident would seem to give them credence. However, train journeys and in particular the old-fashioned small compartments that were once the usual thing on English trains, are known for their atmosphere. The old photographs above your seats of places visited by the train you were on, were enhanced by the smell of dust that had accumulated in the plush. This was to be torn out and replaced with slippery artificial leather, that could be slashed, but held no secrets. Then the photographs too were removed and innate decorative coloured pictures appeared. Then, as now, this in-between existence of travelling in time and space was inducing to private revelations, rather like a secular confessional.

The man, with whom they shared their piece of space, moving towards a now known destination and to the rhythm of the railway time-table, the 'third man', you might say, was very good-looking. Slim, with curly dark hair and elegant. He sported a waistcoat. 'Sported' describes the way he moved to show off this piece of clothing at its best. Training Anna in pronunciation, he leaned forward to show the position of the tongue and the teeth, then leaned back, stretching out on his side of the facing upholstered bench, his tweed jacket opening, and an amazing cream-coloured waistcoat coming into full view. In his beautifully modulated voice, even his 'Pwllheli' sounded gentle, he told Anna, on hearing that as a child she had danced in a *corps de ballet*, that he, too, had wanted to be a ballet-dancer, and there was no *corps de ballet* where he could start. Instead, he had studied economy. His listener's admiration for higher-education made her impervious to the bitter melancholy in his words:

"I am a chartered accountant."

"Oh that is a very good career," she said. "I hope my daughter will be a lawyer, or a doctor. I am doing everything I can to give her a good education. That is why I am here on the way to a better-paid job..."

"Don't choose a career against your own inclinations," he intervened as if appealing to this woman, older than him, to make the right choice, in spite of the fact that she was long past the age of such choices, and whose inclinations were all about earning good money. His appeal went unheard by the hard-working mother who knew what was best for her child in this difficult world where women especially had to keep their wits about them if they were not to be taken advantage of. But his message was heard by the silent child, and though not fully understood at the time, was remembered.

Pwllheli. What a word! What a place! What magnificence of landscape! It really must have been "One of the most beautiful spots in Wales", as the railway poster had promised, though it was not for the scenery Anna and her child had come. Yet there was the sea and there were the mountains. They were in North Wales, where the children only spoke Welsh and where their closest neighbours were a prolific family of rabbits, and you never got close enough to them to know what they spoke. It was beautiful, it was in pact with Nature, and it was lonely.

Yet it is not the loneliness that comes first to my mind. It is first of all the image of a mother busying about a large country kitchen with darkening corners as the sun sets over the fields that divided the house from the edge of the woods where mother-rabbit and her brood appear as soon as sundown brought quiet and shadows to their patch. It was the small child, sitting at the heavy wooden table in front of the window, which gave a full view of the awaited evening ritual, sitting with her supper, her legs out of reach of the stone floor, her chin level with her bowl of warm milk thickened with chunks of bread, the taste so warm and comforting that it remains to this day. When the first rabbit popped up, the mother, too, would sit down at the table. One evening, through the twilight, they counted eight baby rabbits!

Only after these memories of the sight of the family drama outside, recounted by the mother as a fairy-tale, only after the warm milky taste has settled, only then does the word 'loneliness' come to pervade the quiet of the fields and the kitchen and give voice to what had been soundless.

Looking back, it was a beautiful time.

Beauty is perhaps always a lonely thing.

The road from the green meadows and mountains of Northern Wales to the grey pavements of London was long and winding, each turn fraught with hopes and disappointments, and another notch in the money belt, a few more twigs to Anna's nest-egg.

It started with 5 Harley Wood, Nailsworth, Gloucestershire. That was where Anna brought her baby daughter. It was not quite her own home because she did not own it. However, in the middle of wartime rationing and general scarcity she had 'everything'. The neighbours would come in for a cup of tea, and ask to borrow a cup of sugar. Or a little flour. Or a few eggs. Because Anna kept hens and had given up sugar in her tea. She also kept a couple of goats so there was always enough milk, and since her youth in Italy she enjoyed her tea with milk, *all'inglese*. The little Cotswold stone house was falling apart; the roof was untrustworthy and partly exposed. The garden, or rather the small allotment surrounding it and reaching as far as the lane and the fringe of the woods, was Anna's pride. The goats had their area, the hens and chickens were all over the place, the rest was covered with potatoes, carrots, parsnips, lettuce, cabbage, radishes, lines of runner-beans and sweet peas, tomatoes near the walls of the cottage and here and there were dahlias, sweet Williams and French marigolds – a few of her favourite flowers. All succumbed willingly to her care.

How long did she live there? She and her 'no-good' consort must have been there a while before her daughter turned up on the doorstep. Or maybe not. Maybe she moved in with husband and baby girl. A ready-made family, just as it was meant to be. No one must know.

Maybe the Manor was the next stop. The enormous grounds, the gardener and the pond. Alfred William was there for a while. Their quarters were an entire house to themselves, connected to the main house by a brick corridor.

He was also around when they lived in at another manor house, not so large but with a large enough garden to require a gardener. That is where he saved his daughter from the creature in the kitchen cupboard into which she had crept. She liked cupboards. Then she caught sight of the monster-sized spider over her head and screamed. He had come running, relieved to see what the matter was.

"That's not dangerous" he said and swiped it off with a wet cloth.

"It's only a harmless daddy-long-legs."

Then why had he killed it? She had only wanted him to get it out of the way. It hadn't made a sound. It was hardly visible on the cloth he showed her when she insisted on looking.

At that same place, a man passing in a car had rescued her when she got stuck in a mire in her wellingtons. He simply lifted her out of them and they sank. She was sad to lose them as she loved her wellies.

And where was Anna? She was definitely there, working. Perhaps not yet used to the fact that her little child was growing and branching out on her own.

It was at the big manor she had sent him packing. He was making everything difficult for her. He was no help at all. And perhaps he had already begun to use the child as a threat to getting his own way, which usually meant money. "I'll tell her..." "I'll kill you!" The little family became mother-and-daughter.

At the next place of work as housekeeper, it was time for kindergarten and her daughter was picked up everyday by the father of another child and driven there in a pony-and-trap. That was a peaceful time.

Though she was always worried, about money, about the future, about how she was to afford the good education she had to give her child, Anna was in many ways content in her new 'position'. She could see her daughter every day, they had a lovely large room with good furniture, an old-fashioned mahogany wardrobe with a full-length mirror, like in Italy, where her little girl would dance in the silk petticoats her family had sent her. She would never have been able to afford such luxuries here, even if it had been possible in England to buy that kind of quality or style. She knew, too, that the child liked going to 'school'. The four-year-olds were in the same building as the school proper, and were weaned to the transition. As for example being present in Assembly. However, Anna did not like some of their disciplinary methods. One boy, who had done something wrong, unspecified, was made to pull down his short trousers in front of the entire school and thrashed. The father that drove the trap told her. All the children had been very quiet. It eased her worries about her growing daughter talking to a father who himself had two children, and it would have been no help to talk to Alf, he was no father, and no husband. He only made trouble for her, and she was glad to be rid of him, even though it meant that she was now a 'woman alone', unprotected except in name and status. The child enjoyed pre-school and when they rolled out their mattresses in the middle of the day to rest. You did not have to go to sleep but you had to lie quietly and close your eyes. She had begun to dread starting at school proper. It seemed so large and strict.

They were good people, Anna's employers. Their children were older and away at boarding school, so they had time to take *her* child with them on different occasions.

Mr. B. took her for a ride in his car, but they had to stop because she got sick. They had probably given her something that did not agree with her. On the other hand, she, Anna, was always sea-sick. She was already beginning to forget the genetic gap.

It was true English countryside, and Mr. B would take the child on exploratory expeditions. He showed her where the blackbird had nested in Spring and how to recognize the pale green-blue brown-speckled eggs. He even took one and showed it to her, with great care. It was tiny in his man-size hands. Then he put it back and told her never to take an egg from a nest or there would be no more blackbirds to sing in the trees. They went back there every day until all the eggs were broken and the nest was filled with gaping red throats and yellow beaks, and the mother bird flew back and away and back all the time to fill the squeaking young.

Once, even though Anna did not like the idea, he took the child on one of his bird-shooting trips. He told her to squat behind a bush and not to move, only to watch what happened. He huddled there too until the dog, an Irish setter, started quivering and stood alert, as they do in pictures of hunting scenes, its wet nose twitching into the distance. Mr. B whispered something to his dog, and she ran off, nose to the ground. "Watch" he said and all at once a large bird flew up from a bush a little way off. But he did not shoot it. Or was it that the child did not remember? She remembered the excitement, and the warm masculine closeness, the smell of damp tweed and the shining trembling dog.

Where was Anna's next stop? Was it near Stratford-on-Avon? The picturesque village with the Tudor cottage with its garden and gardener, where the Colonel's widow lived with her only son, who at the time was in the Army, and whose father had been an ardent collector of butterflies.

She lived alone in her spacious rooms and welcomed Anna and her child. The child, at home in the outdoors, quickly found the company of the gardener, a man of few words and of great patience. She also threw herself at the owner's two dogs, a cocker spaniel and a black and tan dachshund. Especially the dachs, being smaller and younger and amenable to play. To a point. And the little creature bit her lip in the middle of a passionate embrace. Her mother cried, afraid that the scar her lovely little girl already had incurred on her mouth in an accident earlier would be reopened. The undaunted daughter, however, continued to pursue dogs of all sizes for the joy of those trembling slobbering signs of affection mixed with the unexpected danger of attack. The dogs' owner, though often having to reprimand the child for her unlimited love of dogs, like feeding them secretly at the dinner table because she could not resist their imploring eyes, their owner had taken more than a liking to her and told Anna that she wanted to do well for her. In fact, she would like to adopt her. What irony for Anna! Her subterfuge had succeeded so well that she was looked on as the 'real' mother. And what a dilemma! For she too wanted to do her best for her child, but did not have the means at her disposal that her employer had. Her dilemma ended with her strengthening her determination to manage on her own, but that meant she had to move on.

Was Cheshire the next stop? The Catholic widow, who became Anna's next employer, was childless and she too wanted to adopt her housekeeper's daughter. She understood that Anna had no one else, and that this child 'was her life' and instead promised to provide for her education. Maybe Anna herself finally understood that no one was going to turn up and take her child away from her. That she was in fact the mother. At last, she could settle down for a while and concentrate her earnings on the purchase of a house, in time. Her daughter was enrolled at the nearest Catholic school and was driven there every morning by the chauffeur, who picked her up before lunch and drove her back for afternoon lessons. There was no time to make friends. For the child it was a kind of Limbo, though not knowing either Hell or Heaven, while for Anna it was close to perfect. Perfection however is the end, when there is no more to add or to take away. A dead-end, so to speak. And not compatible with human life.

Anna must have forgotten that such a state could not possibly last.

The lovable Catholic widow fell ill and died. She had not yet made her Last Will and Testament and her nephew did not feel obliged to carry out her intentions and provide for his aunt's prodigy. Nor did he need the services of the Italian cook, notwithstanding her excellent references, and his aunt's desire that she be given a position. He wanted to be fair, but after all, she had only been in service there for under a year. Anna solved the problem. With her notice and her wages she was ready to move on.

Although these changes happened quickly it was not a sudden death. The process of dying took time, a time where the child was brought in to the lady's bedroom to talk, or be talked to, in a soft and loving manner, and to receive careful embraces. To the child, she looked like a different person from the shadowy grown-up around the house or discussing the menu with her mother in the kitchen. Her silky grey hair was plaited and bowed and lay on the pillow, giving her the appearance of a grey-haired young girl. And when she kissed her cheek, she felt how incredibly soft the old lady's skin was, as soft as it was white. That sensation remained forever in the child's memory and under her fingertips. And there was the picture of an open coffin in a dark entrance, alone. The child peeped over the edge and saw her benefactress lying there in a pale silk dress and the white skin with a rosy hue. She looked better than when the child had last seen her in bed. She looked more alive.

Those few moments were very quiet. Until a worried nephew rushed in and drew her away.

Away. Away. Which way, Anna? The Malvern Hills? To work as companion-cum-housekeeper for the pianist who practiced left hand scales only, for hours every day. The pianist had a beautiful view from her windows and a beautiful garden, and her neighbours had beautiful gardens. The neighbours received many eminent visitors, mostly musicians, among them Stravinsky, a serious man who kept his eye on the path as he slowly walked in the grounds, while conversing with the neighbours and the accompanying child. The left-sided pianist and Anna talked about him a lot. There was much grown-up talk in that house. The pianist was not interested in children and thus the child was free to roam all over the garden, and from garden to woods, to search for any company she might find. She found a shy mole. His fur was so soft, so silky. She would keep him and care for him in a little suitcase under her bed. He would be her furry friend. The child had a room of her own, with a window looking straight out on the garden, and the wood. She would sometimes have nightmares where an intruder, fleeing out of the woods would climb in that window and would attack her, but her uncle in Italy turned up in the middle of the night and saved her by covering her bed with rifles. She forgot all about her mole. The grown-ups found it after many weeks, following the smell.

The War lived on in people's minds.

And there had been wars before around the British Camp where the pianist practiced her scales. The Wars of the Roses had an air of romance and mischief about them to the unwitting youngster tangled up in adult conversations. The last stand against the Romans by Caracterus was less light-hearted. But she knew nothing of him or of his capture by his enemy or of his journey to Rome as a prisoner or that he had impressed the Emperor Claudius so much that the Emperor gave him a house and a pension! Did Anna know about all that? None of that was apparently true. Except that he was indeed taken prisoner by the Romans, and probably at some other place in the vicinity. *Se non è vero, è ben trovato!* But Anna would have believed it and turned it round to demonstrate the generosity of the Roman leader. This was while she was still struggling to save enough for her house, and had not yet reached the age when she could claim her pension.

The official from the National Health Authority came to her there at British Camp to fill out the forms necessary for her to apply for this pension. He was young and meticulous. He could not believe Anna was over 60, even though it tallied with her birth date in her British Passport. Someone might have made a mistake and he could not risk making another. He insisted very politely that he had to have the original birth certificate from Italy and that it had to be translated and given an official Italian stamp. All this official interchange must have taken place and ended successfully as Anna in time received the pension, for which she had worked so hard.

For her daughter, watching and listening, Italy became a real place, not just somewhere else, far away. Her mother *was* a foreigner, born 'abroad', which at the time was an exotic place to most British Islanders.

Foreign-looking papers with foreign writing and an excess of stamps eventually arrived by post. However, the unreality of distances prevailed in the childish mind until nearly 60 years later, she saw with her own eyes the entry in the Church register in Gallicano nel Lazio.

Nearly forty years had passed since she last had been there, in this medieval village perched up on a ridge pushed up between two rivers, making it the perfect choice for safety from intruders, and the whole area amenable to the aqueduct system developed by the Romans. Anyone wishing to enter this bastion would have to pass through an arch from the east or another arch from the west. There was only one street and there was a church at each end. In the past forty years the need for defence must have dwindled, and new houses spread themselves out beyond the Chiesa di San Rocco. The people of Gallicano built this church in the 17th century because their prayers and promises had protected them from the plague that raged all round them. The Church was erected outside the main habitation, to protect their vineyards and olive groves, their livelihood and their future. Today the newer houses start from this point.

The heart of the place was unchanged. The old centre was intact, the fountain where it had always been in the medieval wall, though the water had dried up, and from the steps of a later fountain and memorial you could see out over the whole valley below. An inscription in indelible ink had been added later, much later: *When the doors of perception are cleansed, things will appear as they truly are: Infinite. W. Blake.* Then added, just under, in the same writing, but hardly legible: *Everything that has a beginning, has an end! Matrix.*

It is curious how places you have kept in mind for long periods of time appear shrunken when you actually revisit them. You would expect the opposite, given that the image in memory is somehow lodged in the twisted turns of the brain, a piece of matter filling only half a head. Some say this phenomenon is due to the fact that when you are a child everything is disproportionately large. In my case, I was not a child when I was last here, yet all the houses, steps, the walking distance from one end of the street to the other, had lost so many of their dimensions as to become almost unrecognizable. Are all memories like that? Inflatable reality? Is nothing as we think it is? Or is everything just as we think, and we turn and twist it as we please, using the mirrors of time?

I had no recollection of having before entered the Chiesa di Sant'Andrea, though obviously I must have seen it. There had been a church on this site since 1100, pulled down and rebuilt in 1732, by a wealthy benefactress. The Baroque façade was a surprise on the small medieval square, and the interior was even more surprising, giving an impression of enormous space. The heavy church candles were lit, and the candlelight increased the height and depth of the darkness, a point of fire and life among the disappearing shadows. A funeral was soon to take place and large decorations of flowers made me feel I had stepped back in time to other older celebrations.

The spaciousness had been reserved entirely for the church itself. The step from the vestry to the offices where all church records were kept were narrow. The slabs were worn down deeply in the middle, and steep. I followed the Father into a tiny office, for which he had first to find the key, and was left there while he completed his preparations for the funeral service. He was preoccupied yet did not hurry me, nor himself. Finally, he had placed the ledger for baptisms from 1875 on the heavy oak table, after pulling out first two Volumes which proved to be the wrong ones. The table took up the entire room, leaving hardly any place to move about in, in front of the bookcases full of similar ledgers, all locked behind glass doors.

He carefully turned the pages to the entry I was looking for, excused himself for a few minutes and left me alone to decipher the lines written over a century before.

The writing was neat and slanting, with few intervening spaces. Each child inscribed was allotted six lines, it seemed. The ink had faded, but certain downward strokes were still ink-logged. I could hear the scratch of the pen, dipped in ink, tapped against the lip of the inkwell, slowly moving across the page. That hand that held that pen had long since lost its skin and muscle and become just bone.

As I again looked about me I imagined the thousands of names written here in these books. They filled the dusty little room with quiet. Once, these names had sounded in the streets outside. That morning, no sound from the street penetrated these thick walls. I felt I was sitting in a bubble of history.

The priest came back and helped me read entry number twenty four: *D'Offizi, Paulina Anna Maria,* with the date written out in full, the last words looked like 'twelfth of June', which was when the child was baptized. He waited while I photographed the open book and then suggested that he make me a photocopy. As if he had all the time in the world.

Again and again, in the years to follow, I have pored over this copy, and the names registered there. The father, Eleonoro D'Offizi, the mother, Josepha D'Aquilio, the god-mother, Magdalena D'Aquilio, and a couple of names which are illegible. And with her naming began her life, and thus her death, as for us all. And her true survival. Her name has not disappeared though faded in ink, though twisted and turned and crystalized first into *Nina* and later into *Anna*, pure and simple, one of those words which appear in complete balance with themselves, even when seen in a mirror. Her birth was her vanishing point. And for this vanishing point to be the turning point of another view, that tiny hole large enough for a human eye to look through and to see the same image but in a different way, to distinguish what was real, - the object or its image-, for her to vanish and to reappear, for her story to be told – she needed me. There is, however, no future in writing, on paper or in print. It only underlines what is past.

But a voice, unrecorded and still heard, in the ear rather than a middle point in the head, her voice, a mother's voice, not to be rendered on paper in written words, is a presence that can be summoned at will, proving the future as the eternal present, to be grasped one second at a time, and lost in the present, death inevitably comes closer, becomes more familiar, loses its horror. *Horror vacui.*

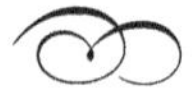

7

Anna was not afraid of death, she was afraid of dying. Of pain, of dying alone.

And she did not want strangers washing her body after death.

Worry kept her darkest fears away. Her constant worry about health and money, or rather lack of it, kept her going in her life project: giving her daughter an education that would ensure her a future of independence, whether as doctor, lawyer or playing the piano at the local pub. She had slaved for others and her free spirit had suffered. She laid her plans for the future, for when she no longer was on earth to take care of things. She was afraid someone, who had no right to do so, might lay claim to the remains of her worldly goods to the detriment of her daughter.

I remember clearly our visit to the solicitor, when she made her Last Will and Testament. His office was on the second floor of the corner building, just across the road from where we were living, over the ill-fated tobacconist shop next to the gasworks at Vauxhall. I must have been about fourteen. It was the year of the Hungarian revolution.

His office was dark and small and full of untidy folders, as one expects solicitors' offices to be, reflecting long drawn-out litigation, even though the prospects of closure were not as bleak as in previous centuries.

Her Will was a straightforward affair as wills go. Nevertheless, her ideas on the legal profession and her experience of human nature had made her aware that any ambiguity could have Dickensian consequences.

She wanted it made absolutely clear that all she owned was to be left to, 'her only daughter'.

"Your *adopted* daughter."

The solicitor was also interested in clarity before writing anything down.

As a mere statement of fact, it sounded simple enough. To me, it had a strange echo. As if it were of someone else she spoke.

I had known for several years about how I came to her, which was in fact how she came to me, and had decided not to mention it again before I felt she would be able to give me some answers, but it was as if forgotten, by us both. By her, in the undercover tone she used when she had to repeat the solicitor's words, there was to be no misunderstanding as to my status, and by me, in that I did not recognize myself in 'my adopted daughter'. I felt I was a bystander, yet the label hung on me like the name labels tied with string hung round the necks of London's child-evacuees, sent on trains to avoid the German bombs. The words remained long after the war like sticky buds from country lanes.

That morning in the lawyer's office was the one time I heard her pronounce those words.

When all was, so to speak, completed and the solicitor was about to call in the witnesses to Anna's signature, she stopped him and said she had not finished. There was her husband.

"I want to leave him sixpence."

The solicitor looked abashed.

"You don't have to leave him anything, madam."

"He shall have sixpence. I want him to have sixpence. Write it down."

And this was duly added to the document, the daughter embarassed at the solicitor's discomfort, understanding that this was not usual procedure, and not understanding that the man and the child were both witnessing a relatively civilized expression of Renaissance fury and vengeance, as yet unleashed.

Anna left in great spirits. I just wondered, and remembered.

Sixpence. Half a shilling. After the disappearance of the farthing, the small round of silver was the smallest coin in use in England. Anna used to sing *A Song of Sixpence* with gusto:

"I've got sixpence, Jolly, jolly sixpence.

I've got sixpence to last me all my life.

I've got tuppence to spend, I've got tuppence to lend, and tuppence to take home to my wife – poor wife."

"Ah!" she would add.

"I'll show him who is 'poor'!"

If she had lived long enough she could have heard her song sung by Nick Cave and the Bad Seeds, and though Nick Cave does not have the kind of melancholy in his voice that would have appealed to her, she would have picked up immediately on the Bad Seeds. Alf was a bad seed.

"He was good for nothing," she used to say.

Yet in the solicitor's office, she had not even considered him good enough for *that*. He had to be given some token of smallness. 'Nothing' was boundless.

King Lear was known to her only by name, but had she known him better she would have commiserated with his plight. This unquestionned expectancy of the rewards of filial love, unbelievably unrequited, was too much for a parent to bear. She would have been blind to his blindness and as deaf as he was to the sound of the love imbued in his dearest daughter's proclamation of how she vowed to fulfill her duties to him. In fact, the latter would have sufficed as love itself. But Anna wanted measures of the immeasurable, just as Lear did. He had to have all, or it was nothing. He did not understand what he was asking for. He was left with not a thing, when his two other daughters started to measure the needs of one, no longer king, nor father for them.

Perhaps in that far off time when Anna had sought love's measurements and been happy with her daughter's three sacks, maybe she had unwillingly trapped me into never giving her her due.

The child had answered too quickly, too ready to appease an unknown judge of weights and measures, succumbing unwittingly to the seductive tyranny of numbers, encapsling her love in time, until it was too late.

Anna, even so, displayed a different understanding of these matters when not duty bound. She understood that she could not leave Alfred William 'nothing'. 'Nothing' was the size of space, endless and eternal. That was much too much. Sixpence was just right. Which was more than Lear got in the end.

Yet, he might well have received sixpence. Not the real Lear, the Lear of the Celts, who was around before the Romans came to the foggy island, but the Lear we know, and who is as real to us today as he was when he prowled the Elizabethan stage. Sixpences had been already coined fifty years before the mathematics of his counting-house of needs, and his all-or-nothing idea of love, had turned his mind into a madness, where with Cordelia dead in his arms he embraced love and death as one.

The little silver coin was a lucky charm, sown into the jackets of RAF airmen in the Second World War. And a charm for brides, too, on the threshold of another perilous enterprise. Brides are still trying their luck, while the War is over and won, though not luckily for many of those men. The year Anna died they stopped making sixpences. Alfred William lived on for another seven years. Long before that time, he had already faded into oblivion, and never got his sixpence.

And *you*, Anna? Paulina Anna D'Offizi, Nina, Mrs. Sheldrake, that "bloody foreigner", what did *you* get in the end?

You got back to your beautiful and beloved Italy, to "those who really loved" you. Much was changed. Your loved ones were no longer alive. To you, in exile, they had lived on in your memory, ageless. Again, you were disappointed. Thirty years had passed.

And from the world?

Not much gain there. Yet you kept faith in your own soul, that you had done what you believed to be right. You had been a friend in need, even to your enemies. You did not expect anything in return. Except acknowledgment.

Anna was a woman of two worlds, 'beholden to none', avoiding any debt, especially that of gratitude. If someone did her a favour, she would do them two. If she received a gift, she would give one of greater price. Her generosity endeared her to people. And she was generous. Nevertheless, deepest in her was a terrible fear of being trapped by what another might consider she owed them. It was a question of independence, of freedom. Her two worlds were two eras. She still retained the conviction that a woman alone was a difficult and dangerous one, fostered as she was in an Italian village at the end of the nineteenth century. A woman needed a man to protect her and take care her, thus proving he cared for her. In her other world, she was a radical, a conviction derived perhaps from the same village roots. This conviction had evolved early from her sense of justice and from what she saw of injustice about her, and in trying to comprehend the world of music and the opera, of the ballet in all its beauty against the backcloth of the screams and the silence of the dismembered bodies of war.

Balancing distances in these worlds meant she could only unburden her heart to the few, to her daughter, to a priest, or to a nun. To those whose duty it was to listen. Respect for the order of things. was patterned in squares, circles. numbers. And no returns. Apart from a certain peace of mind.

Outside of the drawn-up lines, outside of your control, everything was worry.

What did the world see?

A strict woman, yes, severe even. Yet at times amazingly open to argument from those she respected and whose respect meant something to her. As the time when the Italian café- owner near Vauxhall intervened, when Anna was about to send off, reluctantly, her teenage daughter to the pictures with just enough money for ticket and bus-fare.

"Give her a little extra. She's 16. She should have a bit of money in her pocket."

He was a man, who resembled Anna's cousin, Cesare, in his laid-back view of the world. He might have been sitting at his proprietor's table with its practical oil cloth in any small town in Italy, outside on the pavement near the café's entrance, smoking his cigarette down to his fingertips as he philosophised on street-life passing and on life in general. Only the scenery, or scenario, was changed, as he sat there in his sunless kitchen, in an as yet not pulled-down construction in the shadow and sound of the railway bridge.

The daughter expected to hear the usual stirring dramatic tale of the hard-earned wages which would put the brave Italian in his place. But no! Her mother mumbled something, he replied, mumbling more emphatically, and then she gave her daughter 5 shillings and an admonition.

"Don't spend it all - on nothing!"

The world would also see a proud woman, full of self-confidence and dressed up to the nines when the occasion warranted it, a visit to the building society, or to a lawyer. She would invariably cause a flutter with her Italian elegance in London, on the wrong side of the river, her musquash fur coat and cloche hat, her high-heeled booties and fine leather gloves. Her coat and hat were long outdated. Yet through her attire shone a self-confidence in her own attractiveness that gave her an aloof look, bordering on arrogance. The old body with its middle-aged spread still poised itself proudly like the ballet-dancer it had been. Anna's tiny feet were now marred by bunions after many years restraint in elegant Italian shoes, but she had kept her slim ankles and legs. She exercised daily as if she had danced all her life.

"My doctor can't believe I'm over seventy," she would say. The doctor being the only man who saw her undressed, and whose expertise must carry weight since he saw many women undressed.

She would move as on a stage, or taking a stroll down a Roman street for *la passagiata*, displaying her beauty as though still twenty, allowing herself to be admired, and desired, but – *non si tocca* -. If a fellow should be daredevil enough to approach, a single glance would cut him down. Until then she was sweeter than sweet.

When she dressed up, it was to her own standards of what suited her, and to her own conventions. She stood out. It was her intention to stand out. She had no desire to merge in with the crowd. At school arrangements, I could sense the flutter she caused and would feel uncomfortable, as if *I* were the one out-of-place. Which, in a way. I was. Anna was in her element. She was indeed at home where ever she was. Unflinchingly.

She stood out at home, too, though less conspicuously, because less public.

At home it was sensible to wear well-used clothes that were comfortable and easy to do housework in. Anna, however, never ceased to suffer from the exigences of the cold and damp English winters and was confronted with the problem of wearing enough clothing while still being able to move freely. Her solution was newspaper. She would line her chest and stomach between her woolly vest and jumper with sheets of newspaper, inevitably crackling a little as she moved about. She understood that visitors, of all ages, could hear the unexpected sounds and readily revealed her patent to them. The younger ones tried to hide their giggles, which did not offend Anna. This was just the result of their ignorance.

"That's how I keep my health in this country," she would explain.

Any tramp would corroborate her claim concerning the insulating properties of newspapers. Of the various Sunday papers, which were on the whole larger than dailies then, she preferred the *News of the World*.

"It is a good size. And thinner."

Also, the same one she bought for the crossword and to study the horses.

Her interest in the races kept alive her memory of her father. Race horses had been the reason for his visits to England. *Her* interest was whether they could earn some money for her. For this, she studied form. The all-purpose table in our living-room-cum-kitchen was covered with cuttings, which showed the placings of certain horses over a long period of time.

"This one is going to win this time!" she announced, and was off to the bookmaker.

This too was an occasion for full attire. He must not get the idea that she was a poor creature in need of money. Whether he thought that or not, he groaned when he saw her coming. She inevitably won. Small amounts, because she also took the safe bets with high odds, not only to win. Later, she tried the same system with the pools, without the same success, but usually breaking even. With a drawer full of cuttings on the football league, she possessed an incredible knowledge of the teams and their players.

Let it end there. With Anna's collection of plans and dreams.

ANNA

Anna-

Here is your story.

Though not only yours.

The story I promised you I would write.

What would you say, if you could speak to me now?

'*What* can *I say?*' is what you used to say when presented with the obviously unchangeable.

'*You are not my daughter. And after all I have done for you. But one day when I am no longer here... Then you will be sorry. Then you will cry your eyes out. Then it will be too late.*'

I don't understand my daughter.

After all I have done ...

Well, never mind, God knows

She *will* understand. I know that. She is not stupid. And I have given her a good education.

And what is all this she is writing?

It is rubbish.

It is not about me, about all that I have done and have sacrificed for her. I made many sacrifices so that she would lack nothing. It was wartime, everything was rationed, meat, sugar, flour. My coupons were first for her, then me. Before I got her, I smoked forty cigarettes a day. I gave them up at once.

I wanted a little daughter and it was the war, so I thought I would do some good for this country that had saved me from Mussolini. He was a good husband and father and many lies were spread about him, but he was dangerous for Italy, politics are all dirty. Anyway, I wanted to have a little girl who could look after me when I was old. So the Adoption Office showed me this beautiful baby, only a couple of weeks old, whose mother had had dark hair and brown eyes like me, they told me. I never met her. I didn't want to, she was a bad woman. I'm sure she was Irish. I didn't want to know anything, and they said it was a healthy family, which is the most important. I wanted her to look like me. She was to be *my* daughter. Alf did not want her. He said we could have a child of our own. What did he think! I was 53 and I was not going to love him. I had refused a baby to Enrico who was a good man, and for whom I would do anything, only not *that*... But I told Alf nothing. I kept all these matters to myself, my fears of a man's body. That started when I was very young in Gallicano, the man in the woods, and my mother's pain after the birth of my youngest brother who died I can't remember how young he was – two maybe three – and how she contracted peritonitis and died. *Povera mamma.* Alf could not understand these things even if I had told him. I let him believe that one day, maybe, I could have a baby with him. And he had to promise that he would never say a word to anyone that my child was adopted. No, he said with a kind of smile. Or I would kill him. He understood that I was not joking.

She was 2 months when the court made her mine. She had been named Jean Patricia in the Baptist faith, so I changed her name and baptized her a Roman Catholic.

Marie Josephine, was the name I chose for her. My grandmother was Guisepina, and the Empress to Napoleon, a great man, an Italian, was Josephine. I like the French name, it was the same in English, but I used to call her *Marie José* before she went to school. Alf did not like it. Though he seemed fond of her and wanted to make her the same as all the other children and English like him. He even made me cut her lovely long plaits when she was 3 and a half. He said she looked very nice but I cried and saved her silky hair in tissue paper in my trunk. He always made things difficult for me.

When I brought my little baby home at last so that I could look after her myself, I got a shock. All her little body was covered with sores. *Madonna!* What had they done to her? The first months I had to bathe her with olive oil and cotton wool, while I cried all the time. I washed her with my tears! But I never let her cry. If she cried I would pick her up straight away and change her or feed her. I couldn't bear to hear her cry. "Leave her to cry," said the health sister or people visiting. Never, never would I let my darling cry.

Povera figlia abbandonata!

And I don't understand these mothers who leave their children alone. Why do they have children if they do not want to look after them? Yes – I had to leave my daughter alone sometimes, but that was because I had no choice. I had to work to keep us both, I had no husband, only a man who was good for nothing. Except to use my money. And it broke my heart every time,

When she was old enough I found a good Catholic boarding school for her with nuns who looked after her and I paid them well. Also for extras like piano lessons. Not riding lessons, I would have been worried all the time that something might happen. The uniforms were expensive, but of good quality. Especially the white poplin shirts.

Every time I accompanied her to a new school, or brought her back to a new term, I tried not to let her see me cry. It was terrible for me to leave her there. She looked so small. And I couldn't bear to visit during the term – then I only suffered more. My friend who drove me said I should leave while she was in the dormitory collecting some drawings she wanted to show me. I cried and cried but I think she was right. She was a good friend to me.

The nuns understood me and told me she would be fine with them.

I promised myself that one day when I had saved up enough money for us to have our own home, I would keep her with me always. I would never leave her with anyone else again.

I missed her every day and even more in the evening when I had finished working. "You should go out sometimes and enjoy yourself," people, friends, would say to me, even when she was a little baby. How could I enjoy myself if my child was at home without me. "A baby-sitter," they said, Alf too. What is that? A baby-sitter? No one can replace a mother.

And when she was at boarding-school I worked all the time. I could not visit her very often, but I made sure her school was not far away from me so I could feel she was close to me. The school in Ross-on-Wye was a very good one. That is where she began piano lessons and the gardens were beautiful. Many of the pupils had rich parents who could afford all the extras but I did what I could and I had to save as well for the future. She could not come home for the week-end like most of the others. There was no real 'home' to come to. But the nuns were very kind, the St. Joseph sisters, like her name-saint, and they looked after her, I know.

My Marie made her First Communion there. Then I went. I knitted white cotton stockings for her to go with the white dress and shoes. The same as my mother made for me.

She did not want to wear stockings, she wanted three-quarter socks. But everyone had those, I did not like them. They were for boys. She cried a little, but they looked very nice on her, like a little princess. I cried too. I had worked to make those stockings. And I cried from joy. All those small children in white, saying their prayers and the nuns singing. Oh what memories! Afterwards all the parents and children went into the nun's sitting-room and the tables were covered in white damask and with bowls of strawberries and cream. It was beautiful. I was very moved. When I left, I thanked Reverend Mother for everything she was doing for my daughter, and told her how much it meant to me and that she pray for me. I took her hand and kissed her ring, that is what we do in my country, to show respect. My daughter did not like that. But she is too young to understand. She has to learn.

It was a pity she had to leave that school.

When I used to finish my work, I only wanted to go to bed to sleep. When you are a living-in housekeeper, you have no privacy. It's not your own place. When we were at the pub in Middlesex, my employers were very nice to me and my daughter. They would invite me to their own sitting-room over the pub to watch the television – not many had television then in 1950 – but we just sat in the dark without speaking so I was so tired I would fall asleep. Is that enjoying yourself? In the school holidays my daughter would go in and watch with them. They would watch something called *The Scarlet Pimpernel* which she liked but she did not understand always. After all it was for grown-up people, and she was afraid to ask. She asked me, but I did not watch it and I said she must ask the husband. She was shy and did not want to interrupt, she was a considerate child, and that is why everyone wanted her. He told me it was about the French Revolution and explained to her what was going on. It was complicated for a little girl. But there was not much for her to do there. They were very kind people, however, I could not stay there. I wanted to buy a house in London and I had enough money saved for a mortgage. In London I would find a good Catholic school nearby us and I would let out some rooms so that I would not have to work so hard. I was not getting any younger and could apply for my pension.

When I bought Crewdson Road I was so happy. At last I could live with my darling. And I found a good school for her and she got best marks. I told her you must always look at those better than you. I was very proud of her. But I did not tell her often. The same as my parents with me. You can always do better, I told her. And she was practical as well. She painted the kitchen when I was in bed with pneumonia. I was very ill but I did not want to go into hospital, and leave her alone. She nursed me.

So young. I was her age when my mother died and I had to look after my sister.

They were good times. But she changed.

When she got older. She became cheeky, and talked back to me when her friends were there. Yet she had some good friends, and I think they understood me. I could see they did not like the way she talked to me. Making fun of me. Well, she was not Italian. If she had been in Italy she would not have dared to behave like that. No respect. I told her I was a mother in a million. And what did she say? "Thank God for that!" I don't know what she means, but I told her she would regret it someday. No one would ever love her as much as I do. She would understand when she was older and had her own children, and then she would cry her eyes out.

I couldn't stay in Crewdson Road. There was not enough money coming in and I had three jobs. Even after I got the house free of the other tenants. The last one, the old woman, was difficult. It was my house, I had worked hard to buy it and she was paying almost nothing for her flat. Which was larger than where I was living on the ground floor. And she turned everybody against me. But I showed them who they had to deal with. I sold it in the end to a West African, someone my lodger Gloria from Jamaica knew. A very nice man. The neighbours did not like that. They thought they were better than anybody. He did not mind. He had a large family and many friends. He was pleased to get such a large house. He paid me enough so that I could buy a small tobacconist. I was fed up having other people in my home. But I had to work 16 hours a day, again. And it was not a nice area to live in with a daughter. Vauxhall. The Railway and the Gasworks made it very dirty. And the traffic. As a business it was in good spot on a busy corner. I did not take the offer I got because I was sure I could get more. I made a mistake there. There were no more offers. So I had to find someone to help me out of the mess. I found a very nice little place in Solon Road where it would be lodgers again, but it was too expensive for me a woman alone. I accepted the offer of this Mr. William X. – I can't remember his surname. He wanted me to call him Bill, but I don't like that. He had good plans for making money and he thought I would be his partner in other matters. When everything was signed I made it clear to him that we were to have each our half of the house. He made a lot of trouble for me, getting drunk and coming back late singing loudly and calling me bad names. My daughter told me not to go out of my room and shout at him and maybe she was right. I might have killed him. He did not frighten me. It was unpleasant for my lodgers. And his tenants did not stay with him long. In the end I let my half and moved to Cavendish Road, near the school and rented two rooms in a lovely villa and did not have to work any more. I won a little on the horses. It was more difficult with the Pools, but I always got back what I bet. The horses, I understood and studied how they had done in previous races in the newspaper. I looked at the ones with high odds and placed my bets according to how I thought they would do this time, if they were on the way up. You have to think like the jockey. I always won enough to give us a little extra. The bookmaker did not like it when he saw me coming!

It was a good time. Except my daughter was changed. She did well at school but she could always do better, I told her. And she had many nice friends. I liked them very much and I preferred they come home to us. I was always nervous when she was out, some of them lived far away on the other side of London. The streets and Underground in London are not safe for a young girl after dark. Good girls should not be out then. She and one close friend got scholarships to stay 3 months in France to learn the language properly. They had to find families where they could be paying guests and they could not go to the same place. She was gone for nearly 4 months. A friend of mine said she did not understand how I could let her go, at 17, alone. For her education I could put up with everything. She came home in October, brown and healthy. She had bought herself a watch, like mine, the one an admirer had given me in Italy and which she had lost. I am sure her friend at Primary School had taken it. We spoke French together the first days – I had forgotten so much. I had a little job then in the West End at the fur-shop where I had worked when I first came to London. She came in to visit me, and they asked her to wait in the showroom. When I saw her I was so ashamed. She had come in the rain with no umbrella, no stockings, like a gypsy, and gold ballerina shoes which she had bought in the South of France. And the green suede jacket I had made her buy the last winter because it was good quality. Everything was wet, dripping all over the beautiful soft carpet where the customers and models were. She looked like nobody's daughter. I told her afterwards.

The next summer, finally, I had enough money to take a holiday in Italy for the first time in 25 years and to show her my country and my family. After all she was not 'nobody's daughter', she was mine. She had to finish school so I went one month ahead and when she came we went 3 weeks to the sea in Anzio, which I remember from my youth. Then she could see for herself what a wonderful place it was. Nero had his summer palace there. She stayed on the beach all the time, even when everybody went away for lunch she stayed under her parasol reading. She could not get enough of the sun. I think she understood then what the sun was, and what I had missed all those years under the grey skies.

Her fiancée John and his friend from the Salvation Army came to visit there. And John stayed with us when we went to Gallicano. He was a good man. From Scotland. I had been in Aberdeen once. He was from near Edinburgh. I told him about my life. I did not tell him my daughter was adopted. Reverend Mother told him. She had no right to do that, but it did not matter. Perhaps he would understand better what I had sacrificed for her. He gave her a lovely ring. Like a rose. A ruby with diamonds around. But she was too young. On the other hand, I did not know how long I would live, I wasn't getting any younger, and he had a good education as an accountant. Now he wanted to be a schoolteacher. They do not earn well. Whatever happened, he would be able to care for her.

He came with us to Gallicano.

I did not like it when they went for walks in the woods near my village. Everybody can see everything from the village, which overlooks the valley and the woods. Cesare my cousin said I was too strict. But I did not like it. In public. So I kept her in doors. For her own good.

When she went back to England before me to start at the College, I wanted to stay, at least until September, a woman came to visit me and presented herself as the mother of Gianni. She was so pleased to meet me and to talk about her son, who had won a Bronze Medal for swimming in the Olympics in Rome. I did not know any Gianni. She said he wanted to marry my daughter and that he had met her on the beach. Nothing improper had taken place. He was impressed with her, his mother said, and had written to her in England, in Italian because he did not know much English. I told her it must be a mistake. My daughter was engaged already. She was very upset and I felt like a silly fool. I was very angry. When I came home I told my daughter what a difficult position she had put me in. She had misunderstood several things he had written to her, but I don't understand her at all. This is not the way I brought her up. And before I came back she had broken off her engagement as well. She did not want to talk about it, but I saw she had been crying a lot. She was the one who did not want to be engaged, so I don't know why she was crying. Well, I thought then it was for the best. Soon, I did not know any more what was for the best.

She could go to Italy and work, I told her. There was a couple, I met on the beach, who wanted her to live with them and teach English to their children. A very nice couple and she could learn Italian properly. She could get a good job as an interpreter. With languages you can get anywhere. I didn't want her to work hard like I had to. No. She did not want to be an interpreter, she did not want to live in Italy. She would take her secretarial course first and then go to University. Maybe. If she still wanted to become a doctor, I told her my cousin could train her, he had his own clinic in Rome. No. She did not want that. I told her that before, when she finished school and was engaged. But then, no. She wanted to marry and work as a private secretary. Well, a private secretary was not a bad idea. She would earn good money. As she said herself, the course was only one year and at university it was 3 and a half. For English and French. She already knew English and French. What was there more to study. I wanted her to be a lawyer. When she was determined to be a doctor at school before Advanced Level, the Reverend Mother made her change her mind. I had spoken to Reverend Mother about my position, that I was getting old and Reverend Mother explained that to her, that it was a very long education and that there was still lot of prejudice against female doctors. The prejudice was not my argument. Many people preferred to talk to women doctors. But the important thing was to change her mind, when she would not study in Italy. Reverend Mother told her she should study Literature and the Art teacher, I forget her name, wanted her to go to art school.

She was clever at many things, my daughter. I did not want her to go to art school because of the people there. She said there were people like her there. She knows nothing yet of the world. Artists are like *la bohème*. No morals. She argued with me. But she did not want to go there anyway. She would always draw and paint. She wanted to do everything. Ah, well. What could I do?

I did not expect her to be engaged before she had finished her education. And I did not expect her to break it so soon. But she kept to her plan for the secretarial course. That I approved of. Typing and shorthand in English and French would always come in useful. We agreed on that.

When I came back she had already given him back the engagement ring. He had bought from his friend who came to Italy with him. The friend had broken his engagement before. Maybe that was a bad sign, though the ring was very nice. And she had already been one month at the College in the City, Moorgate. She was out every evening and I was at home alone, worrying about her. I could not rest until she was at home. My friend Mrs. Cash said teenagers were like that and talked to me about her own daughter. Not good girls, I told her.

She had a Swedish friend she met at the College and he moved nearby us from the other side of London. He used to follow her home. Which was something. Then, one Saturday morning two of his friends came unexpectedly, carrying the tape-recorder I had bought for her. He had died in an accident with the gas-heater in his lodgings. The boy who did not speak English had found him. They had shared the place.

They came in and we all sat in our one room. What was there to say? I did not know this boy. These other boys I had never seen before and my Marie said nothing. She was like a stone. What did he mean to her when this came as such a shock? He was not her husband. Not her fiancé.

Well, she had many good friends who took her out with them. I could not speak to her, and to me she said nothing. Nothing helped.

Then she started to go out again. To art galleries like before and to concerts. Again too late in the evenings. Sometimes she stayed at home. Once she decided all of a sudden to keep an appointment she said she had forgotten. I was worried.

I saw immediately she was different. I knew she was pregnant long before she told me. She thinks she can hide anything from me. But I have lived too long for that. I can see everything.

I told her to go to the doctor. That she was too young to have a child. She had been to the doctor. She did not want an abortion. It was against her morals. *Madonna!* What morals! Well. We must make the best out of it. The father was pleased and wanted them to marry. He was from Norway. That is far from me. I think she just wanted to get away from me, after all I have done for her. The important thing is that he is a good man and from a good family. His mother and his brother came by plane to the wedding in June. One aunt sent snowdrops picked the same morning near Oslo. Another aunt sent a bracelet like one from a Viking woman. These gestures mean something to me. That they are thoughtful people. But I can't bear to see her go. It hurts to think she will be so far away from me. I did not think my old age would be like this.

The wedding at St. Bede's Catholic Church was beautiful, the sun was shining and Father Sullivan was a good man. He explained everything to Christian about the children and not to interfere with their upbringing as Catholics. I could see he would do his best and his family. Colonel Green was there, the father of her school-friend, like her own father. If I had had a man like him, my life would have been very different. We went to a private flat in the West End afterwards. A rich friend of Christian lived there. It was very elegant and we could stand outside as well. It had a small private road. It reminded me of when I lived in Via Margutta when I was young, like her. *Ah. La vita!* I had bought the best champagne and me and Marie we shared a bottle to ourselves. It was a very special occasion. And the last time. After all, she was leaving me.

I could come later, when they had settled, she said. But what would I do in Norway? Cold, and strangers. Another foreign land. Everyone spoke English, Christian said. But I longed for my own people, the sun, the grapes, wine and good food, - *la mia bell' Italia!* I longed to go back.

Well, my daughter came to me in London the next summer, to help me sell the house. She had my grandson with her, of course, she could not come without him. Giann'Andrea, a good name. In my family too. Andrea was an old distinguished name. They were the only passengers on a cargo boat from Oslo. Nothing for me, but she said it was fine and that one of the sailors had given the boy a little monkey. There are many kind people in the world. He turned six months when he was with me and had his first tooth. He was such a lovely baby. It broke my heart to see him leave. When you have children the pain never ends. They leave you one day.

Then she moved alone with two children to the North, even further away from me than before, because then I had returned to Rome. I invested in a flat, otherwise the money disappears quickly, near San Giovanni in Laterano. Cheap, because the tenant was still living there and she would not move out. I had to go to court to get her out. She was my age, how could she plead that she was too old to move? I needed a place to live, too. Always the same story. When you are a woman alone, they try to take advantage of you. But I worked hard for my money. What did she think – that she could live on my property for nothing?

I took a job as a companion to an old spinster who was in a wheel chair. To save what money I could. A lawyer is expensive as well. I needed help at my age. If I was still young it would have been different. You should have seen me then...No one could get the better of me then!

One summer, I cannot remember if it was 1966, or '67, Marie came to visit me with the eldest, Giovanni Andrea, he was 4 or 5, a beautiful boy, blue eyes, fair hair, like an angel, everyone looked at him, in the street, on the bus, in the park, but he was not very obedient. And she did not correct him enough. He was not a bad boy, he was a boy and he must learn, or she will regret it later, I told her. She did not agree that he was disobedient, and some things he had to learn himself. Well, later she will remember my words. I found a room for them with a friend of mine, near me, a sailor who now had a boarding house with his wife. He took them in his car to *il Lago Bolsena* and they had a nice day in a little boat. It was so hot in Rome in July. And she had told me about her heart. *Madonna.* It was like a knife in my chest. And soon she was leaving again. I didn't know what to do. She said she was fine but I saw the scars from the operation.

We went to the Zoo with the little boy. Such a happy child! Oh, what will happen to him and to the other boy, who I have not seen yet, if her heart fails? It is terrible to be a mother. Pain, pain, pain. I cannot do anything. They live far away, or I could help her. She should live with me, not far up in the North Pole. She says it is beautiful there and she can work and has help in the house. But I don't believe everything she says. I know she does not like it when I worry. How can I control that! *È mia figlia – senza più di pace.* No rest when you are a mother.

She sent me a little money when she could, and I sent her a wool shawl I crocheted for her, my thoughts for her in every stitch. I wrote her many letters. I tried to persuade her to come to me in Rome:" here, you have everything, fruit, wine, sun, all you need...". It was not so easy, she said.

When she moved back to Oslo with Christian, they all came by car to visit me for a holiday. They have no money. I don't know how they manage. But I cannot interfere. They lived in a tent. In Rome! One thing, is the sea-side, at Orbotello, but in Rome!. Two small tents, like gypsies. I couldn't tell my friends that. I said just 'privately'. They were even sick and had to run to the lavatories all night. And they told me like telling a joke, laughing. I don't understand these people.

I was living at the *Istituto S. Margherita* then, a private old people's home but with no privacy, I can tell you. The nuns were not kind, some yes. They reminded me of my aunt who had to be a nun because nobody would have her, not because she was ugly, but she was spiteful. When we visited her at her convent when I was a little girl, she would pinch me when my mother and father were not looking. I had blue marks all over my arms.

Well, to Christian the Home was a shock. I could see that. For me the place was not bad with large gardens, though they were brown and dry in the middle of summer. It was the people in it that made it bad.

I think for him it was the dormitories, like a hospital where we were 20 to 25 old women together.

"You must come to us. You cannot stay here" So, I thought, maybe he's right. After all, I don't have many here anymore. Except my niece, my grand-niece, she is very good to me. She is the only one. And I am not getting any younger. I do not want to live alone. Maybe it is better in Oslo, with my family.

"By plane it only takes a few hours" they said. I had been in a plane before, once, when I was young. In Brighton. It was a demonstration and the pilot went round and round. The plane was upside down! I said:'Never again!' It was not the same this time. I was afraid. But it was a large aeroplane, very smooth, and comfortable. When I got to Norway, the immigration doctor asked me if I had any illnesses. No. I was very healthy for my age. I had to tell him that my doctor in Italy had told me I had cancer in my breast, and as I was going to leave I should get an operation as soon as possible when I came to Oslo. I did not want to tell my daughter, because I did not want to worry her. She had enough to worry about.

For the first time in my life I was in hospital. I was so afraid I would never wake up. They cut off my breast and told me it would be fine now. After the operation, I felt very weak and I did not understand what the nurses said. They were good to me, but I wanted to go home to my daughter. She looked very tired when she visited me. I should not have said to the doctor that I knew I was sick before I came to Norway. The State could not pay for the hospital bills. I do not know what they can do, they have no money. And she has a bad heart. Everything is difficult. I shall help her with the boys when I come home. She says I must not think about it, that I must rest. What else shall I think about? I can see she is crying.

They had prepared a nice room for me in their flat. Quiet. I made friends with the neighbour Mrs. Svendsen. A very understanding woman. A widow. She helped me to learn some Norwegian, so I could go myself to the little shop round the corner. *Kefir* was what I liked and I felt it was good for me. I managed. I liked learning new words and to be independent. I try to call the boys by their names in Norwegian: Johan Andrea, I say, and Alexi – why not Alessandro. I can't remember these 's' at the end. They know who I mean. I usually have some sweets for them in my apron pocket. Alexi likes that. Johan Andrea does not always want. He does what he likes. I complained to Marie about it. But she does nothing about it. I feel he is cheeky to me. She says he does not mean it like that. I am not respected. If it had been in Italy – That would have been a different matter.

She gets very irritable with me. I think she is trying to make me ill. I am in the way to her. I am afraid she is poisoning me. I have written to my niece in Rome and asked Mrs. Svendsen to post the letters. I have told her why I have to ask her to do this for me. She took the letters. But she did not believe me and gave them to my daughter. She said her mother had been the same way. What did she mean by that? My daughter was very upset, and angry with me. I don't know who to trust any more.

Father Dahl, I trust. He understands me. When they were all away one summer and I was alone, I put the big chest in front of the door. Fortunately, it was the third floor so I could have the window open. In case someone should break in to steal, and kill me. Because I cannot defend myself anymore. He understood that my daughter was away at work so much and left me alone. He said I might be happier with the nuns, then there would be someone there all the time. He arranged it all. She did not want that, but he persuaded her it was for the best. I would feel safer there. It was not far off, near the middle of town and the nuns were mostly Polish. Some spoke French but not English, only Polish and Norwegian. It was nice for a short time. There was a small back garden, which soon felt like a prison with high walls around. And only old people sitting there with nothing to say. It reminded me of the *Instituto S. Marghariṭa* only smaller. The same nothing. And no sun. I shared a room with only one woman, a Norwegian. She was nasty and complained all the time. *Chè miseria!* No peace any where. My poor father. What would he think of me now?

She did not visit me often, even though it was not far from her school, and she looked worn out all the time. Old before her time. I thought when I made every sacrifice for her education that she would not have to work so hard like me. I don't know what to say to her. There is nowhere anymore to feel at home. Father Dahl is a saint. I kiss his hands when he comes. *He* comes to see me. I can see some of the others here are envious, I don't care. It has been like that all my life.

The day I was sure was my last, he was there and gave me the Last Sacrament. When Marie came, I was feeling better. She was asking me strange questions. I did not know what she was talking about. I only know she is *my* daughter and I have given up everything for her, I took to me when she was a tiny baby covered in sores, I cried every time I cleaned her little body with olive oil and cotton wool. I cared for her. She was mine. She *was* mine. She *is* mine. I don't remember anything else. I don't understand why she is like this now, asking, asking. She is upsetting me. I want to die with peace in my heart. I have been a good mother to her. Given her everything. Everything she wanted. I would do without myself. And a good education. She has not had to work hard like me. I took any job that paid me well. I wasn't afraid of work like some English. They complained when the Italians came and took their jobs, but they did not want to do those jobs. Italians work hard for their wives and families. I wish she had married an Italian. We could have lived in Italy, it would have been a paradise for all of us. *Un sogno.* Everything is too late now. Maybe the Father will come back today.

I am very tired...

REST AT LAST

On 23rd December 1969, Anna died.

The day was cold and overcast spreading a grey light on everything, faces, streets and snow during the morning and midday hours, until early darkness fell, and artificial lighting set us free from the daytime shadows, turning them blue.

She died early in the morning, and was laid out in a narrow room adjoining the convent-chapel. What looked like a cell had been transformed into a funeral parlour, where the family could see her for the last time.

The sisters were accustomed to death and the dead. They had washed her with care and dressed her in pale silk. Her face, devoid at last of all worry, was as smooth as that of a young woman, as if, for a few hours, she had once more become 'Nina'.

But she was not there.

Not Nina, and not Anna.

Her absence filled the room, mingling with the grey outside light that filtered through the window high up on the bare wall. This light and her absence, in some inexplicable way, thickened the air and made everyone appear to move in slow motion, through a mist.

To the daughter, they were all far, far away – the husband, the two children, standing round the bier, and the two nuns, two dark and silent birds, ominous and protective at the same time. Only her mother's face shone clearly. And there was no one behind it. It was as if mouth and eyes, the dark chocolate-brown eyes, had sucked all the the earth's energy into a black hole and then closed themselves, leaving us dangling in space. The intimate smallness of the room, the lack of air and life, the sheer unexpectedness of death made her dizzy.

Her husband held her arm to steady her; her two sons looked at her with curiosity, and at their grandmother in the coffin, lying there peacefully.

"*Nonna's*' only sleeping", the oldest said, seeing nothing to warrant such crying.

His mother cried even more, envelopped in the endlessness of that sleep.

The door was opened uncertainly and another nun came partially into the room. She was flustered and apologetic at the same time. She had a different time schedule from that of death and grief.

In the ordinary course of events in these matters, the open coffin would have been placed in the aisle of the chapel for a short lit-de-parade, and the community would then quietly come and go, offering their prayers. But the following day was Christmas Eve and there was much to prepare for the celebration of a birth, a birth which itself was outside Time.

The nun, who had come in, embodied our restless lives, where between the beginning and the ending of our time zone, we press on towards short breaks on the way, short respites, short pleasures, only to again push ahead, driven by the call of the Mad-Hatter: "Move on! Move on!"

Anna's little family moved on, to Christmas revels for the children, and her daughter to the dream-state of slow motion through the sticky mire of time before the funeral.

The funeral took place on one of the first days in the new year of 1970, at Vestre Gravlund in Oslo.

It was a beautiful and bright morning, and very cold. All was white and baby-blue as it can be in early January in the North. The only sounds were the crunch of winter boots on the snow, and the guttural gasps for breath that broke up the stifled weeping.

There were few mourners present in the Chapel, but the grief of Anna's daughter made up for a million. She remembered nothing of the ceremony, it was the long long distance to the freshly dug grave that remained with her. The cold sunshine, clean crisp snow making each step sound like a drum, the taste of icy tears that would not stop. All those times in the past, as a child, when her mother was not there, when she herself did not cry, now rose to the surface and overflowed, running into Time's river, swelling it into a flood that crushed every barrier in its way, taking with it a whole life. Deep inside she was empty. All that was left was the crunchy rhythm of the coffin-bearers on the path to the hole of black earth where her mother's cast off body was to be stored.

The squeaky crunch of footsteps on pristine midwinter snow became the coldest and loneliest sound in the world.

LONG AGO

Charles Dickens took his family to Italy in 1844 and wrote down his impressions on the way, sometimes as letters back to England. He insisted that they be regarded as his own personal reflections, of events and meetings with people there and then, calling them 'shadows in the water'.

After travels through France and Northern Italy, he and his entourage descended into the Compagna Romana, a place whose very name used to evoke a wistful look in Anna's eyes. Dickens, however, was in no way favourably impressed by the sight as their carriage, bypassing Gallicano, crossed the plain towards Rome.

"...we began in a perfect fever, to strain our eyes for Rome; and when, after another mile or two, the Eternal City appeared at length, in the distance, it looked like – I am half afraid to write the word – like LONDON!!! There it lay, under a thick cloud, with innumerable towers, and steeples, and roofs of houses, rising into the sky, and high above them all, one dome, I swear, that keenly as I felt the seeming absurdity of the comparison, it was so like London, at that distance, that if you could have showed it to me in a glass, I should have taken it for nothing else."

First impressions can change, as those of Dickens changed.

Anna's first impressions of England were in the course of her life there turned completely around. It was hardly his first picture of Rome that had endeared Dickens to her, and had made in particular his *A Tale of Two Cities* her favourite

Long before she became a woman of two cities, she loved this book, and was an admirer of its author. Maybe it was because she was a woman of two centuries, of two completely different ways of life and could move from the one to the other with alactrity; from upstairs to downstairs, freely with the self-sufficiency of a revolutionary, an anarchist even, belonging above by birth, but below by conviction; a loyal Roman Catholic, with the mind of a Protestant and in practice, in her heart, alone with her personal God, who was on her side.

Anna shared with Dickens his observations on society and its injustices, his indignation and scorn over Man's inhumanity to Man, recognizing, too, in herself the need to put right what is wrong. Maybe his dislike of foreigners slipped her attention. If she did notice it, she would surely have put it down to a weakness that came with being an Englishman.

For her, what I believe was *her* 'golden thread', woven in the fabric of her dress, with which she sallied forth into the world, was his portrayal of a daughter's loyalty to a parent, to a father, and the love between them. Then, there was the enshrinement of sacrifice. For Anna, indelibly stamped on Love: indelible even when barely visible.

LATER

'To dear Mummy' I wrote on the fly-leaf of *The Tale of Two Cities*, when I gave it to you on your birthday a long, long time ago. Or not so long, not so far off in the landscape of all our histories and of *our* lives in particular, yours and mine.

Fifty years have passed since I stood in a bookshop in Charing Cross Road and picked out with care the inexpensive edition of the classic. I was then nineteen and you were seventy-two. I never thought of you as old, but as I approach that age myself I realize that it occupied your mind constantly, and that each birthday sounded a drum in a finale that for me had no sound.

After all this time, not the feeling of time but the fact, I have still my wishes, or perhaps they are only one wish, the same as it always was. Though it changed in form and expression and has again changed, returning more articulately and as strong in its voicelessness as it was in those early years, when undeflected, I could cry: '*I want my Mummy!*', causing you sword-like pain and infinite joy.

Then, with the years many other needs and desires intervened and deflected the sound of my speech, until now, once more, I can cry out like that scarred child at the end of the hospital corridor, when she screamed so persistently that the doctor could not continue sewing her torn lip before he allowed her to see with her own eyes that her mother was there, waiting.

There have been many stitches, and much pain since then.

My dear Mummy.

I wish, how I wish, I could say these words to you, that you were here in front of me in your chair, your body weary after the toil of the day, your mind awake even though you needed sleep, the look in your eyes sharp, penetrating, the frown-marks from an effort to see all, one eye-brow slightly raised in an expression of analyzing skepticism.

I wish, I wish. I wish...

I wish I had been beside you when you died.

That I could then undo the anger at you that had engulfed me two weeks previously.

They called me that day, the nuns, or was it the Father, that you were dying and that I should come.

Before I arrived you had improved a little and lay quiet and awake in your bed which had rails like a child's cot, made to prevent you from getting up and wandering around the convent or into others' rooms. You shared your room with another old woman of whom you were afraid. She was there when I came that day and you were no longer afraid of her. You were afraid of something altogether different. You look pleased to see me, and cried, anxious, apprehensive. You wanted me there at your bedside.

I didn't understand much then. The hardness of youth still protected me. I did not understand the finality of death. Not for those facing it, nor for those left behind. Even though I had met it several times, also my own, escaping it by the so-called hair's breadth.

This was my last chance. I had to know the name of my father.

Twenty years had passed since I had discovered my adoption papers, since we had at last moved into our own home in London together, and papers and mementos were also brought together in one place. I had always loved looking, whenever opportunity arose in a holiday or with another emptying of trunks, at your personal things –there were not many – from your magical existence "before I got you", as you would call that dividing line in your life, which also defined the bond between us. There were the silk dresses from another era, a slim golden evening gown from around 1910, a black chiffon with white beads from the 1920's, a long afternoon dress in cardinal-pink from before the War – the Second - and the sequined white evening purse, the mother-of-pearl prayer book in Italian –(the prayer book and the purse I carried at my wedding, you remember?) an exquisite gold watch from an admirer- (and which I later lost, though you were convinced that my best friend had stolen it in a fit of envy) –the camisoles, an unheard-of word in English boarding schools, edged with Venetian lace.

And then the documents. They looked ancient to a nine-year-old.

You were taking a bath in the kitchen, where we had made room for a full-size galvanized zinc tub. We both enjoyed long baths and would fill more hot water from the kettle kept boiling on the stove for when that first delicious heat began to cool off. *Your* bath-time was a small oasis of time for me too and it gave me an opportunity to nose about like a puppy among your private books and papers. I did not think of it as prying as I did not believe you had anything to hide. It was clandestine and to be fully enjoyed needed the uncertainty of being interrupted as well as the possibility of complete seclusion.

The grandiose Edwardian chest-of-drawers in mahogany, you had proudly secured second-hand and which reminded you of Italy, was in the front-room where we had our bedroom and it was the farthest point on the ground-floor from the bath-tub by the inner kitchen wall.

In the deep bottom drawer I unearthed the mystery. Official papers. From a country court. All these different names, written in by hand. My name. And the names of my mother and of the father who no longer lived with us. Then other names that I had never heard of before. *Jean Patricia* referred to as the infant had been given my name, the name by which I had always been known, the name by which I knew myself. And suddenly I didn't. Know myself.

I read the few sheets of paper again and again. The mother of the infant was named, and no father. A myriad of small mysteries fell into place. The one big mystery was still there. I could not comprehend its depth or its length.

I remember my slow steps towards the kitchen, along the narrow dark corridor to the tiny living-room and on one-step down to the stone-floor of the even smaller kitchen. Heavy steps. My heart was beating loudly, the thin sheaf of papers shook in my hand. You were singing.

Oh, how you cried.

Oh, how you had hoped I would never find out. Not until after you were dead.

Oh, how afraid you were that I would no longer love you.

Nothing I said could comfort you.

But I wanted to know. I craved for a piece of knowledge to grasp onto, something, anything about this other mother and this other father. I already understood enough of the world to realize that since the father was nowhere mentioned my 'mother' had not been married.

Did she know who they were?

A straight-forward question calmed her a moment. Perhaps someone had once upon a time prepared her for that.

No. She did not know my "mother"- "*her*". But she must have been a bad woman, that was certain. She spoke of her in the past tense, killing her off. "Irish".

And my father?

She knew him. He was a good man, but he was married.

For a child burgeoning on the age of righteousness, there was a flaw here. The reputed Irish girl was a slut, while the alleged father was respectable, respected, a good man who had to consider his married position and remain anonymous. My mother did not expect the same moral qualities in both sexes, and his disputable goodness was qualified by his being a man.

Disputable or not, he was mine. His name? The name of the father.

Alan. He was a pilot. In the RAF.

He had died for his country.

She cried and cried.

The water was cold, the soap remnants coagulating on its surface, before she managed to get out of the bath. I hugged her through the warmed towels, in front of the gas-fire in our living room.

I did not cry.

I loved her.

How could she forget the three sacks?

All I could do to keep those sacks from bursting was to promise myself never to question her again about the other woman until I was grown-up and could make my own inquiries.

Then I grew up and made inquiries, which came to nothing. War secrets protected by the Law. And above all the rights of the individual. Until the law was changed in 1980, British authorities obviously did not confer the same rights of the individual upon a child. You always said the English were kinder to their animals.

I was sitting at your bed-side in December 1969. A week before Christmas.

You were dying.

The time had come.

I had to re-open the wound.

"I don't remember..."

"I can't remember..."

"Forgive me..."

"*Non posso...*"

I wish I had asked you earlier, when you still could remember that there was no name for you to remember, that it was a story made up to protect yourself.

I wish I had been older, had more understanding, had grown out of the desperate search for my own identity.

I wish I could have seen that you were grown old in spite of what your father had told you, and had surrendered to the fear of dying.

I wish I could have comforted you, as later I have comforted others. In what I failed to be for you, you taught me to be for them.

But I should have been there when *you* were dying. You deserved more.

They said you died peacefully. Without pain. Pain is what you feared most.

I wish I had been with you.

And you were right. As you often were.

About how one day I would understand.

"…one fine day – you will see."

And how I would cry.

I did cry.

And I still cry.

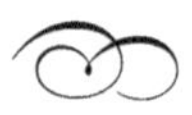

MUCH LATER

This morning, I awoke from a dream. You were standing close to me, facing me, though I lay asleep still. "You are mistaken, you know," you said, softly, calmly, with no haste. "I was always proud of you. Whatever else..."

I felt the cool linen of the pillow under my cheek, felt it cool and smooth, an alien sensation though not separate from me, an image arising of the soft skin of a lady who died long ago and whom I hardly knew, far away in another country, in another life.

But it was not her soft skin I felt. It was my mother's cheek that I could taste and smell under my tender childish kiss. Yet, not her cheek. It was mine. And I was lying in my own cot-like bed, alone, afraid and dying. It was not me dying, yet it *was* me. I was her and I was dying, and it was lonely, and cold.

Then, the shivering baby body was picked up, gently, firmly, and brought close to a woman's yielding breast.

Slowly, warmth suffused them both. Surfaces melted away, leaving only the tenderness of the years, the years of memory and all the years before.

Anna Sable was born in Cheltenham in 1942. She has previously published two novels *The Gilded Butterfly* and *Across the Void.*

CPSIA information can be obtained
at www.ICGtesting.com
Printed in the USA
LVHW090852290919
632602LV00001B/85/P